C000124975

Wounds of a Super Hero

by

Andre Pereira

Wounds of a Super Hero

Book Cover Designed by: Rebecacovers on fiverr
Bonus Poster Designed and Created by: Giulia Davis
Insta: @giuliadavistattoer
Bonus Poster 2 Designed and Created by: Emma Jocelyn
Insta: @emmajocelyn_tattoos

A Copyright has been registered with the Library of Congress.

Positive Zero Publishing

ISBN: 978-1-949541-04-5

Positivezeropublishing.com

To The Reader:

First of all, thank you so much for picking up this book and giving it a chance! Secondly remember if you aren't doing well mentally, or have potential triggers within any topic involving any sort of depression, that's ok. You can put the book aside, take care of yourself. I want you to feel good and healthy. This novel, perhaps more so than many others of mine, will heavily deal with deep depression/trauma.Z

Acknowledgments

For everyone that has shown me support and kept motivating me to keep going, a huge thank you! For the artists that created the bonus posters, thank you so much for putting your vision and work into it! Humans over AI anytime for art.

"You either control your mind or it controls you."

-Napoleon Hill

Chapter 1

The woman sitting in front of Liam was pretty attractive. Stefanie's legs were crossed as she observed him with a gentle, sweet smile. It made him feel comfortable, and he considered it a good thing. He didn't give her anything past thirty. Even then, he thought she could be in her late twenties. She had solid green eyes, which watched him from behind the lenses of her glasses.

She held a notepad in her left hand and a pen in her right. She held the pen close to her lips, allowing Liam to get himself situated. They had just gone through a lot of tedious paperwork, from his information to sign a privacy agreement and his insurance. Liam's attention then shifted around the room.

The room was the size of an average bedroom. The lights were dimmed, but not to the point that it created any darkness. Light filtering curtains blocked the outside light. The temperature was reasonable, good enough to feel comfortable in either a t-shirt or a long sleeve shirt.

Stefanie sat relaxed as she stared with various emotions at the man in front of her. She was intrigued, shocked, and excited all at the same time. At first hand, the name Liam Lewis would not have meant anything to anyone. After his quick confession, however, it meant much more to her than anyone would ever know. Liam had been known to the world not long ago as Faceless, a superhero. Faceless had defeated various super-powered enemies. He had been around for five years, yet there were toys and TV shows explicitly dedicated to Faceless. Almost every day, there would be something on television related to him. Small groups of anti-Faceless had also formed during that time. Liam had never revealed his identity. Thus some debated the legality of his actions. Everyone would know him by his costume. He had worn a blank steel mask, which is why the news source referred to him as faceless, and the name stuck. Then all of a sudden, he just disappeared without a word. That had been two years ago.

It was hard to believe that the man in front of her was that person. For starters, he was twenty-nine, the same age as her. She had always anticipated that Faceless was older, maybe in his forties. The man looked as if he had not slept in months. He had all the signs of someone who was not doing well mentally. Physically, he still appeared fit and capable. He had neglected to groom himself. His beard was a complete mess, and his hair didn't seem to have been washed for a while.

"Maybe we should start as to what brought you here today," Stefanie said in a calm, gentle voice. Liam remained quiet for a bit. Instead, he took the time to admire some artwork hanging on the walls.

"We could talk about the art too if you'd like," Stefanie continued, noticing the subject of his gaze. There was another moment of awkward silence. Liam played with his fingers, his head down, and his body hunched.

"Nightmares," he said softly. Stefanie inched closer, interested and intrigued.

"Nightmares? What about nightmares?" She casually asked him.

"I hear screams. Everyone. Children, parents, grandparents, husbands, and wives. It keeps me up at night, every single night."

"Are these the screams you had to hear back when you were Faceless?" Stefanie asked as she wrote down a few notes.

"Yes. From the battles I had with other super-powered people. Houses destroyed, people caught under the bricks and all other destruction, never to breathe again," Liam continued.

"But they were not your fault, and there was nothing you could have done. Unfortunately, it's not possible to save everyone. The ones to blame are the terrorists that wanted to destroy the world," Stefanie told him.

"It's not that simple. Yes, these super-powered bad people were around, but... but maybe fewer people would have died had I not engaged in battles with them," Liam replied as he covered his face with both hands.

"They made the first move, though. After that, you would come to defend everyone and stop them from causing terror," Stefanie clarified. Liam started shaking his head rapidly.

"It is so much.... so much more complicated than that," he answered. He appeared to be regressing with every word he spoke, barely able to enunciate the words correctly. Stefanie wrote down a few more notes on her notepad and watched him for a few more moments. His eyes were nearly drawn to tears. Stefanie knew that if she continued to press the subject this soon in their sessions, it could end up causing more harm than good. She jotted down a few more notes before turning to look at Liam again.

"Any particular art that you like in this room?" Stefanie asked, attempting to change the subject temporarily. Liam didn't respond; instead, he took a few deep breaths while standing up. Then, just as he was about to walk towards the door, Liam raised his head, second-guessing himself, and retook a seat. His hands were trembling as he took another deep breath.

"Can't say I ever really understood much about art," he spoke while putting his hands over his face.

"Sometimes you don't necessarily have to understand something fully. You can look at it, and you might like it. Maybe you will not know why you like it, but there might be a subconscious reason," Stefanie answered. Liam did not say anything else. Except for the handles on a clock hanging on the other side of the room moving, there was nothing but awkward silence.

"You currently work?" Stefanie asked as she wrote something else down on her notepad.

"I do. I load trucks up. It's more challenging than you would think."

"I'm sure it is. Every job will have its challenges."

"With this one, I need to be cautious of my strength and speed. I need to tone it down not to raise any suspicion," he explained to her.

"I hadn't even thought about that. How do you feel about that? Does it cause even more stress? Or does it help keep your mind occupied with the challenge?" She asked him while once again writing down some notes.

"I'm not sure; I guess I'm indifferent about it. It has not caused me any more stress. Certain things with my powers are easier than others. For example, I am not exactly bulletproof as it's believed. My body has an invisible shield. I could shut it off with my mind if I wanted to; otherwise, I can leave it on as long as I want; it's part of my skin," Liam admitted to her.

"Would there be any particular reason you would want to shut it off?" She curiously asked him. He shrugged his shoulders.

"Not sure. I'm sure somewhere along the line, a reason can be found, but I can't think of any at the top of my head," he answered honestly.

"Have you ever shut it off?"

"Once. I had been curious, wanted to see if I could still bleed."

"You cut yourself?" Stefanie asked, her eyes widening with

concern and worry.

"I did. Just a little, though. I wanted to see if it worked, if I could turn my shield on and off," he responded, looking at his arm and touching a small scar.

"How did it feel afterward?" Stefanie asked as she hunched forward on her chair. Liam began scratching his hair rapidly.

"It hurt a little. I was surprised, to be honest," he responded. Stefanie smiled a little before putting her back against the chair's cushion.

"That's not what I meant. I was talking about how you felt emotionally."

"Oh, well, I was indifferent. I didn't enjoy it, but it's not like I was feeling awful about it," Liam responded as he took a deep breath and stood up. This was the first time in the entire session that he had his back straight and looked directly at Stefanie. Up until that moment, it had been just glancing here and there. She was smiling, the kind you could tell derived from kindness.

"Interesting. Would you like to talk about how you acquired your powers?" Stefanie asked him. He let out a small laugh; he was unsure if he wanted to talk about it.

"I was twenty-two years old at the time. It was about four months after the very first supervillain made himself public. Sheesh, it sounds so silly out loud. Who would have ever thought of talking about supervillains outside of a comic book or a movie," Liam said softly.

"But it's not so silly. It happened. What else are you to call them?"

"Perhaps super terrorists? After all, they all did cause terror. But, I guess now that I say it out loud, saying supervillain or super terrorist doesn't make it sound any different," Liam continued.

"You don't have to feel silly or wrong in here. Just say whatever you feel most comfortable with," Stefanie affirmed.

"Alright, well, about four months after the appearance of the first supervillain. I could see how terrified the world was becoming. How terrified everyone was, including me. I had always felt capable of doing something more like there was another whole calling for me. So I managed to one day follow this supervillain out somewhere. I'm quite surprised that I didn't get caught. I guessed that he was overly confident that no one would be crazy enough to follow him. I ended up in some factory. It turns out it had been turned into a lab run by scientists deemed too extreme for anything official. They worked on special serums. Because they were working outside the legal system and on their own, they didn't have to follow any regulations. I think that's how that very first supervillain came to be. They used him to rob money and more money so that they could continue their experiments. Anyhow, I sneaked inside and found myself in a room with a few serums lying around. I grabbed one. I intended to bring it to officials and let them handle it from there. On my way out, I was caught by one of the scientists. He then called the supervillain to dispose of me. Rather than outright killing me, he injected me with the serum when he came. He told me I would die within an hour or days without the controlled environment and additional necessary treatments. He dropped me off in the woods, where I remained there, barely able to breathe. I didn't die, though. After that, the rest is history," Liam told her. Stefanie, in shock, wasn't sure what to say and instead remained silent for a few minutes attempting to process it all.

There was an understood silence in the room. Stefanie hadn't intended it to be rude or neglect Liam, but he understood that it could be quite a bit to take in all at once. She nodded a couple of times as if talking to herself in her head. She was about to say something but then stopped. Liam forced a smile, yet it still felt gentle and genuine.

"It's alright. You don't have to feel bad. I said a lot already, especially for my first day," he told her, hoping to ease her mind.

"I am so sorry; I didn't mean to be so quiet. Feels a little unprofessional," she quickly responded.

"I don't think it's unprofessional. This is unprecedented. I'm sure there were no courses on dealing with someone with superpowers," Liam joked, and she smiled.

"That's good," she told him while feeling remorse.

"What is?" He asked, confused.

"You were able to joke a little; we can work with that," she replied.

"There are times I feel a little better than others," he admitted.

"Have you found any possible correlation between better and worse times? Anything that could be triggers for each?"

"Not at the top of my head, no," he quickly responded, leaning back on the sofa.

"That's fair enough. Perhaps something to keep an eye on. You could write it in a journal when you see a change in mood. Maybe it's something you saw, maybe something that happened, just an idea," she told him.

"I will keep that in mind," he responded.

"We don't have much more time left, so I just wanted to briefly go over what I was thinking for our next session. First, we can go over what your focuses are when it comes to your therapy sessions. Then, we can keep working on re-framing thoughts and ideas. How does that sound?"

"Sounds good," Liam told her disappointingly. He wasn't disappointed with her plan. Instead, he felt disappointed that the session was ending for the day. Somehow he had gone in stressed and anxious but had managed to find himself more comfortable and at ease.

"For next week, then, what is your availability like?" Stefanie asked him. Liam scratched his head for a second, trying to recall his schedule.

"I believe I am off next Wednesday, much like today," he responded.

"Do you want to do next Wednesday at five again? Perhaps earlier or later?" She asked him as she looked through her appointment book.

"Five o'clock seems fine with me," he responded. She nodded and then started to write down their next appointment.

Liam's mind went into deep thought as he started to recall the very beginning of the day. It had been a couple of weeks since he had initially set the appointment to come. However, as he had woken up that morning, he had begun to have doubts that he would even show up. He had spent most of the day keeping his mind busy going from store to store without even buying anything except for a coffee.

He had shown up at the building filled with anxiety. He had located the room he would be going in on the second floor. At that point, he had contemplated with himself just leaving the building. Since he had made his way there fifteen minutes early, he would have time to. His stomach had turned and twisted until the time came for his appointment. Stefanie greeted him with a smile and a soft tone. Even when they had been going over all the paperwork at the start, she had never made it feel like it was all business and just about money. She had been kind and gentle with her speeches and questions.

It all brought them to this moment. The session had lasted longer than forty-five minutes, yet it felt as if it had flown by. He stood up while preparing to leave. He grabbed his coat from the couch and put it back on.

Stefanie also stood up with her constant smile. She put aside her notepad and appointment planner and looked at her newest client, who no longer appeared to be as reserved as he had been when first walking in.

"Well, it was nice to meet you. I will be seeing you next week at five o'clock again. I hope that you have a good week," Stefanie told him as she walked towards the door to open it for him.

"Thank you. I appreciate your time, patience, and kindness," he truthfully told her, followed by a bow of his head.

"That's why I'm here, to help as much as possible," she answered kindly. She was slightly shorter than Liam. He gave her maybe five feet, six inches, considering he was five feet eight. He bowed his head in her direction again and then walked out of the office. He found his way to the stairs just down the corridor. He slowly made his way down one step at a time, as if he wasn't rushing to leave the building. However, he knew it wouldn't take much to find himself in a dark cloud again once he left the building.

Everything great always seemed to end up going that path. First, it would give him an adrenaline rush, and then it would all quickly crash, and the cloud would return. But, if he had questioned before, he knew he'd made the right choice to show up. It was the choice to seek the help he desperately needed.

Despite all the positive thoughts and pros he had taken from his first session, something gave him the feeling that it would somehow not fully solve the problem, that one way or another, the cloud was there to stay with him for the remainder of his life. He hoped to be wrong, but skepticism still seemed to prevail. He opened the door leading him outside to an uncertain world. He glanced back once more as he sighed, and out he walked.

Chapter 2

The night had still been young after he had left his therapy session. Unwilling to return to his tormenting place called home, Liam decided to go to a store. He had walked inside with his usual serious expression. He was relieved that the site was pretty empty, except for a couple of families shopping with their kids and a few young couples. He walked to one of the stationary aisles steadily. He looked at the journal section, remembering Stefanie's words that he should start writing down details from when he felt in a better mood and when he was feeling worse.

He started looking carefully at all the choices he had. All of a sudden, he began to feel overwhelmed and stressed. Who would have thought there would be so many choices for a journal? He picked through a few of them, opening them up and getting a good feel for how they felt. A journal had never explicitly been something he had written on before. Did it matter which one he got? For whatever reason, he thought that it did matter. If he were going to be motivated to write on it, he would have to pick just the right one.

He finally decided on one with an intricate blue cover; the pages were beige. He didn't know why, but something about that particular journal grabbed his attention the most. He kept it in his hand as he walked to the movie section. He began to look through the selection. He felt like it kept getting smaller and smaller with each visit he had. The digital world was something he had mixed feelings about it. In one aspect, it would eliminate potential waste. Still, in another, he didn't get to have that exhilarating feeling he always had when holding a new book or movie. He peeked through the section, but none seemed to catch his interest.

He then decided his shopping was done. He walked up to the front of the store, where he saw a line building up toward the only open register. He elected to use the self-check-out to get out of the store quicker. Once he paid for his journal, he slowly walked toward his car. The sky was a little cloudy, and the moon was nowhere to be seen. It had become even colder than before. He found his car and quickly entered the driver's seat, where he decided to let it warm up for a little after turning it on. He raised the radio's volume and closed his eyes as he allowed the music to enter his ears, soothing him. He had no idea where else to go, but he dreaded heading back home.

Something about his house seemed to trigger the worst of his memories. Perhaps it was the enclosed space or the fact that he didn't have much else to do, or maybe it was just all in his head. He didn't know what to think of it. Even just thinking about it was giving him more stress. Why did he always do this to himself he wondered. He had been fine being able to talk to his therapist about it, yet now his mind was letting it all go again. He would have to wait another week to be able to go to therapy again. It was a week too long, he felt. Once he felt warm air from the vents, he began to drive away.

Rather than driving straight home, he decided to take a detour. Taking the back roads would not only prolong his drive home, but it would offer a different scenery. One much better than the boring one the highway would provide. The first part of his back road trip allowed him to see pretty big houses; only wealthy people could live in these houses. It was something he knew he would never end up achieving. But, after driving some more, it changed to just average homes. The kind that was more attainable yet still difficult nowadays for the average person.

He felt disappointed when he finally reached his apartment and parked his car in front of his building. He kept the engine on a little longer and sighed in sadness. He knew what was to come, go inside the house, try to figure out how he would sleep, and then work the next day in the afternoon. A cycle that felt like a never-ending loop. He finally decided to turn off the engine and left the car. Even though it was the beginning of March, it was still relatively cold. In a way, it was amusing. He had developed super strength, flight, a bulletproof body shield, and even extra speed. Yet, the weather and cold still hit him the same way as anyone else.

There was no way he could explain it, but then again, there was no way he could explain any of his powers except for an underwhelming explanation of DNA alteration. That was basically what the scientists had told him. It wasn't something he ever found the need to further expand on anyways. Things were as they were, and the explanation was irrelevant as it did nothing to resolve his issues.

He walked into his apartment on the second floor with heavy footsteps. He didn't turn a single light on. Instead, he threw his journal onto the couch in the middle of the room and headed toward the bathroom. He turned on the hot water on the sink and let it run for a little bit to let it warm up. There was a mirror at eye level, but he never looked at it. Instead, he kept his head down, watching as the water ran through the sink.

He reached out to get a feel for the water, which was warm enough for him. He splashed some into his hands and then placed them over his face. Never once did he look in the mirror. Instead, he sprayed his face with hot water while many random sounds played inside his mind. They sounded like buildings being torn apart. He shook his head as if doing so would cause the sounds to fly out of his ears. *But, Ahhhhh*, he began to hear. Screams of many people, women, men, children, the list could go on.

He held on to the sink with both of his hands and started to take some deep breaths. When he heard a slight crackling sound, he quickly let go of the sink. He looked to where his hands had been holding, and sure enough, he could see a little crack. He grunted in frustration; this meant that he would soon have to get another sink. He had already broken two in less than a year and looked to be on the way to number three.

Idiot, you need to be more careful.

Despite having been a superhero at one point, it hadn't made him wealthy by any means necessary. That had been one of his biggest struggles when he was still Faceless. Finding the balance between working and being out there to fight super-powered villains. He turned away from the sink and walked out of the bathroom, never looking in the mirror once. He found his way to his room, where he dove into his full-sized bed with his stomach facing down.

He put his head in between two pillows, quickly pressing them against his head, trying to fool himself into thinking it would drown out the sounds. It did not. Frustration continued to grow, this was becoming a nightly ordeal, and he wasn't sure how much longer he would be able to keep going this way. He had tried all kinds of sleeping aids, none of which had done anything for him.

He let go of the pillows and quickly turned around to look at the ceiling. There was nothing interesting to look at, yet he stared at it intently. He was able to see the roughness of the white ceiling. There was no actual pattern, smoothness, or detail to it. It was as if it had just been painted and put there without a care.

Once upon a time, he had dreamed of buying his own house. He had known exactly what he would have wanted. He wanted a lovely ceiling inside the house. Although it wouldn't have to have been actual wood, he wanted to have the appearance that it was. The house would also have two floors, with an attic and basement. Each floor of the house would have its restroom. His backyard would no doubt have a swimming pool that he could keep warm during the winter, allowing the use of it all year round. He would also have a hot tub. However, these dreams faded after he acquired his powers and decided to use them to take down any supervillains threatening the world.

He looked at his clock on the side of the bed, and time just passed very slowly, and sleep still seemed so far away. Finally, feeling frustrated, he sighed again and decided to turn and face the clock. He began to admire the simplicity of the clock. It was simply an alarm clock that could be found at just about any large retail store. It was a dark blue digital clock in a rectangular shape. He then decided to stand up and walk on over to the kitchen.

His refrigerator was beginning to run low on food. Shopping would be something he would need to do soon. Yet, he had no motivation to do so. It was always the same thing, too many people food shopping, clogging up the aisles. The noise was generally louder in the food area, which also gave him inner panic attacks. It wasn't very reasonable, and he knew it. A bunch of people talking loudly and making noise did not signify any supervillain attack or destruction. Yet, he couldn't help himself and felt like he was running out of air to breathe.

How much longer would he be capable of living a life like this, where his mind had turned into his biggest villain yet. He wasn't sure he could fully defeat it, but he was undoubtedly going to try. His visit with Stefanie had given him an entirely new light of hope. He grabbed the last yogurt cup from the refrigerator and looked at it carefully. It had expired a month before.

Great, way to waste food, you fool.

He threw the yogurt into the trash can and then opened a cabinet door to see if he could eat anything else. Empty, much like his refrigerator. He again sighed, a routine that he was becoming far too familiar with. He then walked out of the kitchen and went to sit on his couch, a couple of inches away from the journal he had thrown earlier. He crossed his arms and legs, maintaining his other foot on the ground, and started tapping it rapidly, like an anxious person.

The fuck do I do.

Frustration was growing, and his lack of sleep started affecting his patience, mind and thinking altogether. He quickly took out his cell phone from one of his pockets and searched for different ways to help him sleep. He wasn't expecting to find the answer. After all, this wasn't the first time he was searching for it. It wasn't even the second time. He had searched it so many times that it was now the first thing that popped up on his search engine. Yet, there was no harm in looking. He may find something new this time; someone may have made updates. In a far more realistic ideal, they would have invented a sleeping aid strong enough for someone with superpowers. Doubtful, however.

After searching for almost thirty minutes, he put the phone away and looked ahead at the television in front of him. At this point, he wasn't even sure why he owned it, considering how little he used it. He would try to use it, but most of what was on television only reminded him of his past. They tried to portray being a superhero as something without consequences, without casualty, and that all the destruction could easily be redeemed. It was all a picture-perfect selling point.

He stood up from his cheap couch, which he had purchased in a shop- an all-retail store, and began to pace around it. He would scratch his hair, waving his fingers around, take some deep breaths, and look in all directions.

He looked at the time again, it was eleven at night, and he had no idea how it had gotten that late already. He wanted to go out and purchase some food, but the closest store to him that would still be open would be a twenty-minute drive. A drive he wasn't so confident he was motivated enough for. He then went into his next plan; a few fast food places remained open late, which may be his best solution.

He went to his car and quickly turned on the engine, and let it run for a bit so that it could warm up. His radio automatically connected to his cell phone and started playing very relaxing music. At one point in his life, he had enjoyed some heavier rock; lately, it was a bad idea. He couldn't explain it, but fast-paced music would depress him. In the meantime, softer slower-paced music helped him relax a bit. He knew this was something he could write in his journal, but it was back inside the house, and he was in no mood to go back in to grab it. Perhaps when he got home, he would write on it.

Once he felt warm air from the vents, he began driving away

from his house. He took a right at the first light he came across but had to stop for a red light immediately. He waited patiently until it turned green, which felt longer than it generally did. He drove until he finally made it to his destination. There were two cars ahead of his on the drive-thru. He waited for his turn, ordered something off the menu, and drove off after paying for his food and receiving it.

Rather than going straight home, he decided to park in the parking lot and eat inside his car. He would find any excuse not to go back to his house. After eating, he laid back on the seat and put his head up. His mind started spinning with thoughts. Since when had life become so frustrating? Seven years ago was his answer. At the same time, he had started being Faceless. He just hadn't realized it until he gave it all up.

It was then that he started having flashes. Flashes that he hated and yet had to live through them every single day. He would see a bunch of smoke and destroyed buildings. The faces of people were all covered in dust, the panic and the screams of the innocent and the laughter of some of the villains he had faced. Life had been much simpler before a group of crazy scientists meddled and created serums that gave people superpowers. It was greed. When was it ever not about greed?

To make the world a better place. That was always the reasoning given by anyone with any terrible invention. Yet, it never made the world a better place; it only enhanced the sorrow within it. Would there ever be forgiveness for what he had done? Although some of him hoped so, another piece of him hoped not.

He looked ahead and decided it was time to go home and, at the very least, attempt to get some sleep. He wasn't expecting much success, but he had to try at least. Every day that kept passing without him getting much sleep, the grumpier and gloomier he became. He didn't want to be this way; he didn't want to feel this way. But Stefanie, she would help him, right? It was her job, after all, to help people. He would need patience; changes like this wouldn't just occur overnight.

He drove back home. He counted at least three police cars that he went by. They had been parked someplace with their headlights on, hoping to catch someone either speeding or drunk driving. Liam wasn't concerned. He wasn't any of them. He didn't even drink alcohol. He already feared what he was capable of without alcohol; he didn't need any more influences to get careless.

It was a short drive, but it had been better than nothing. Liam

19

found his way back to his house, looking at the couch and seeing his journal still in the same spot he had left it. He felt like there had been something he wanted to write on it, but he couldn't quite remember it. Oh well, it must not have been that important. He shrugged and headed towards his bedroom.

I fucking hate you. Piece of shit bed.

He stared at his bed like a frozen statue. His back hunched a little bit, his mouth was a frown, and his eyes were half-closed.

Why don't you just lie down and close your eyes?

Because you are a fucking idiot. Just keep standing here looking at the bed as if it's going to change magically.

Why don't you just shut up?

Well, you are having a conversation in your head with yourself. I think that you are just crazy.

Of course, I am.

Liam shrugged again and then walked over to his bed. Without changing his clothes, he lay down on his bed and pulled up his comforters. He turned sideways and attempted to get comfortable. He then turned to the other side and then back again. He did it a few times until he finally became frustrated and pushed away from the comforter.

Too damn hot.

He switched his position again. His stomach was facing up, and now he looked up at the ceiling again. Except this time, he couldn't see anything, the room was pitch black, and he didn't feel any sleepier than before. Had he ever been able to fall asleep without any issues? It was something he couldn't remember, and it was making him curious. His mind continued to overthink as it usually did. What would he be eating tomorrow? What would work be like? Would it drag out? Or would there be enough work to stay busy and lose track of time? Then he started to hear more sounds of destruction and people screaming. He shook his head while closing his eyes.

Each second felt like an entire hour. Liam lost count of the number of times he kept turning in his bed. He would sometimes grab his comforter, pull it over him again, and then push it away. Finally, he reached the little counter on the side, trying to feel up for something.

I forgot the damn water bottle.

He sighed and got himself out of bed. There were still many sounds in his mind that he did not want to keep hearing. He kept trying to change his thoughts. Finally, he left his room, walked toward the kitchen, and opened his refrigerator. He was then reminded that he didn't have much left, including water bottles. He grunted softly and swung the refrigerator door shut a little harder than he had wanted to. He walked to the sink in the kitchen and grabbed a glass. He filled it with tap water and placed the glass on the table.

'Here comes the hero, faceless. Ha! Ha! Ha! Have you come to fight me? You violent little prick, the voice in his head was of someone else this time. It was a much more high-pitched voice than his own. It was a voice that Faceless knew too well and did his best to try and forget, but he doubted he ever would.

He walked to his bathroom, and without looking at the mirror, he turned on the water on the sink. He waited for the water to warm up before splashing his face with water.

'Kill me!' The voice returned to his head. He let the water get hotter as he splashed more on his face.

'Kill me!' The high-pitched voice continued to yell. Liam closed his eyes and gritted his teeth.

'Kill me! Or I will kill them all!'

"SHUT THE FUCK UP!" Liam yelled out loud and then splashed even more water on his face. His breathing had become heavier, and then he realized. He had yelled out loud. Would the upstairs or downstairs neighbors have heard him? Even if they did, they might think he was talking on the phone rather than yelling at a voice inside his head.

He walked out of the bathroom and back into the kitchen to grab his glass. Returning to his bedroom, he looked at the couch and saw his journal still in the same spot. He thought that this was something he should write down. But, the truth was, he wanted to avoid making an effort to grab the journal and then write in it. He returned to his room and lay down on his bed. He looked at the time, which was nearly two in the morning. It was a little past five in the morning when he finally managed to fall asleep.

Chapter 3

It was eight-thirty when Liam quickly rose from bed just as nightmares consumed him. He took a few deep breaths and promptly went into the kitchen to fill one of his glasses with water. Liam gulped through the glass and then took a few more deep breaths. He only had to work at twelve, so he still had a couple of hours to spare. The fact that he had even gotten a couple of hours of sleep was surprising; better to get some sleep than none.

He checked his phone to see if he had any notifications, which he did not. It didn't surprise him one bit. It wasn't like he had any close friends anyways. He walked inside the bathroom, turning the shower on to the hottest setting possible. He waited until the water became as hot as possible and then jumped into the shower. He stood under the water with his head down, allowing the water to touch his skin and feel the warmth. It helped him relax, and if he could, he would spend the entire day just like that every single day.

With all his superpowers, including the bulletproof shield, he still couldn't explain how he could feel the cold and warmth. He would probably never find an explanation; it would probably make little sense if he did. Then again, he had superpowers like other supervillains in the past; sometimes, things just didn't make much sense.

Liam must have spent forty minutes in the shower before deciding to come out. It had been outstanding. His mind had been cleared, and no thoughts had gone through it. Instead, he tried to find little things to waste his time until he finally had to depart for work.

He made it to work with just a few minutes to spare. He looked around and saw others heading inside with their usual unhappy looks. Some stood outside, waiting for time to pass as they smoked. A few people looked at him and nodded without saying a word. No one enjoyed speaking much before work. Everyone had the same feeling; they wanted the day to be over. Liam was a bit different. While at work, he got to distract his mind from the usual mess. It was a good distraction.

He walked inside the building and punched in before heading to the usual warehouse, where he would be loading trucks for the remainder of his shift. He was the first one back there, as he usually was. Everyone else would take as much time as possible without getting into trouble. It didn't bother Liam. He simply looked at his tasks and knew what had to get done. He grabbed a pallet jacket and found his first pallet to load into the truck.

Shortly after, one by one, the team started finding their way there as well. They all started doing their job, and just like that, a couple of hours passed, and then it was time for their first break. One of Liam's coworkers approached him. This man was around five feet six and looked like a chicken without much meat. His face was oval-shaped with a tiny chin. His nose was too small for his face, and his brown eyes looked reasonably bland.

"Look at that fucking guy over there," the man named Josh spoke. Liam looked behind him to see Brad standing there with his phone in his hand. Brad must have been just under six feet tall. He was obsessed with going to the gym and had nothing else to talk about besides pumping weights. His hair was a blonde buzz cut. His dark green eyes focused more on his phone than anything else.

"Man never does any work. But he's always kissing the boss' ass," Josh continued. By now, Liam was used to hearing everyone complain about everyone. Just as Josh was complaining about Brad, Brad would often complain about Josh. They both would make some interesting and intriguing points. Josh was right about Brad. He spent too much time neglecting work and on his phone, but somehow, he acted like a wonderful boy to the managers. Meanwhile, Josh also liked wasting time complaining about what Brad and others were doing. By now, Liam had learned that the best thing to do was simply nod and not say much else.

"Are you coming to break?" Josh asked him. Liam thought about it for a second and decided it was best to go. Josh was somewhat sensitive; he would take it personally if Liam elected not to accompany him to their short paid break, even though Josh would pretend he didn't care. In the one year that Liam had been on the job, he had learned quite a lot. Josh was in his mid-forties and was having some sort of mid-life crisis. This is why it was no surprise when Josh tried to make plans with Liam during their break.

"Going out to the bar tonight. Lots and lots of hot chicks out there. This bar I'm going to, they have a dance night every Thursday night," Josh told him as he reached down his pocket for a cigarette. Liam didn't care for the smell but remained quiet to respect Josh's choices.

"That's cool," Liam casually answered. The truth was, he didn't care about any of it. None of it meant anything to him. Enjoying his life, and having fun, was not something he deserved.

"Come out tonight! You may find yourself a nice hot chick," Josh told him while lighting his cigarette.

"I think the terms hot and chick might be a bit degrading," Liam pointed out. Josh looked back at Liam as if he had three heads and two horns.

"Huh?" Josh said, a little outraged.

"I mean, there are better and more elegant terms, such as beautiful and women," Liam told him.

"Huh? You fucking drugs?" Josh said, still with an outraged look. He placed the cigarette butt to his lips and began smoking.

"Anyways, you fucking coming?" Josh asked. Inside his mind, Liam was sighing. He looked away for a couple of seconds and then turned back to Josh as smoke blew toward his face. Liam waved the smoke out before finally responding.

"I can't today. I have a few things I need to do, and then I need to go to bed early because I have something to do early tomorrow," he lied. But, of course, he lied; what else was he supposed to do? Tell Josh, no, thank you, it sounds like a stupid plan? He may not be the best at socializing, but even he knew how to filter himself.

"What the fuck you got to do on a Friday morning?" Josh asked as he put the cigarette back in his mouth.

"I have to do personal things," Liam responded quickly and annoyed.

"Whatever. I have a few more buddies coming. Guess someone isn't getting laid tonight."

"Something tells me I won't be the only one," Liam answered in a low voice.

"Huh?" Josh asked, appearing confused.

"Nothing," Liam told him. He looked at the time and decided it was time for him to head back.

"Hey, I'm heading back. I'll see you back inside," Liam told him.

"Yeah, sure," Josh responded with a tone of annoyance. Liam knew he had not only disappointed Josh but most likely annoyed him too. However, Liam wasn't overly concerned about it. He was confident that at one point or another, Josh complained about him to someone else too. Liam found his way back to the back, where he quickly returned to doing his job. Chaz, another one of his coworkers, approached him. Somehow Chaz always managed to have something negative to say. It was never his fault either; somehow, it was everyone's fault always. The man was about the same height as Liam but a little scrawnier. His nostrils were pretty big, and his eyebrows were all over the place. The one thing that Liam did give him credit for was that his complaints were never work-related.

"Yesterday, my girlfriend says I'm a jerk because I didn't call her after work. Come on, seriously? She could have easily just called me herself. Phone works two ways, you know what I mean?"

"Yeah, I guess. Did you tell her you would call?"

"I think so in the morning when I texted her," Chaz answered.

"Maybe that's why she was upset," Liam told him.

"Yeah, but she could have called. The phone works two ways."

"Yeah, but you told her you would call. Maybe she thought you were busy, so she never dialed. Probably was waiting for you to not be busy and call her," Liam explained.

"She could have texted and asked me if I was busy."

"Maybe you could have texted her," Liam pointed out. Chaz gave him a dirty look and then walked away without saying anything else. Liam had found some weird joy in calling him out for it. He was approached by the only two people at work he could tolerate, Henry and Tati. If there was one thing that Josh, Brad, and Chaz had in common was that neither of them liked Henry and Tati very much. Henry was a twenty-six-year-old man full of life and energy. He had messy green hair, which matched his green eyes, but what Josh liked to complain about was that Henry was gay. Tati dressed very goth-like and constantly changed her hair color. It was currently blue. Her eyes were very elegant dark brown. She was roughly five feet three and on the chubbier side. Henry was very slim but with an athletic body.

"Chaz talking about his girlfriend being mad at him?" Tati asked with a smirk.

"Of course he was. When is his girlfriend never mad at him? Why is she still with him?" Henry added.

"Dunno, maybe she has poor taste," Liam casually responded. Both Henry and Tati started laughing.

"You're not wrong about that," Tati responded.

"So, Tati and I were wondering if you'd like to come to hang with us tonight. It seems like we only ever talk here at work," Henry asked him.

"Sorry guys, it's nothing personal, but I've already turned Josh down too. It's just... I don't know... I'm weird, I guess," Liam answered. He felt that with Henry and Tati, he could be honest. Unlike almost everyone else in the building, these two never took anything personally.

"That's fine. We fully understand; you are far too embarrassed to be seen around us," Tati joked and then winked.

"She is just joking. You know that, right? We understand; if you ever change your mind, we'd be happy to have you tag along. My boyfriend won't care either. Besides you and Tati, everyone else here is faker than fake itself," Henry explained. Liam nodded with a smile.

"I appreciate the invite. But, I am sorry, I just don't quite feel ready," Liam explained. Despite constantly being honest with them, he still always held back his biggest secret, his superpowers, the reason he attempted not to go out much.

"We get it; no worries!" Tati answered with a smile. The three of them returned to work and let the day pass by. Liam did as usual during his lunch hour and headed toward his car. It was the best thing for him to do. He wouldn't have to listen to Josh whining about everyone else. It instead allowed Josh to complain about Liam. Anything said about anyone would eventually always make it to the person's ears. Nobody was capable of keeping it quiet. Maybe that was part of the distraction for Liam; at least, he thought so.

He ate a sandwich he had made with cheese and butter and then laid back against his seat, listening to the same slower-paced music. He closed his eyes just to try and relax, and then the images started flashing through his mind again. There was smoke and dust all around him. People attempted to stand up while others were being helped up. A few were even dragging their family members that had lost a leg. Bad idea closing his eyes. He quickly reopened them with a big sigh.

He turned his car off and decided to head outside. He still had time to spare, but he didn't care. He needed to keep himself busy, so he returned and worked until it was time for the last quick break. Josh was quick to approach him.

"You coming to break?" Josh asked while taking out his box of cigarettes. A little behind Josh was another man with the same attitude as Josh, Mike. The only difference between the two was that Mike had a growing beard that looked like it hadn't been taken care of in weeks. Josh quickly looked at Mike while laughing.

"This guy right here does not want to play with girls, ha, ha." It was typical of Josh, thinking he was funny with his offensive words, but Liam found none amusing. Liam had always thought of Josh as a middle-aged misogynistic man who believed himself to be cooler than he was. So it was sometimes tempting for Liam to say something. Still, he knew it was best for everyone if he avoided any kind of confrontation at all.

"I think I'm just going to work through my break," Liam answered. He noticed the annoyed look on Josh's face. Josh headed out with Mike, leaving Liam on his own.

"Can you believe this? Now my mom is texting me about why I haven't texted her in three months. So, mom, why haven't you texted me in three months? The phone goes both ways, people; they're all about themselves," Chaz told Liam as he approached him.

"Should it matter who texts first?" Liam asked.

"That is not the point, Liam. The point is, why it's always my fault? Do they not know how to operate a cell phone?"

"Do you always reach out to them first?"

"Not always, no."

"Is your mom mad, or is she just wondering why you haven't texted her in a while? She could just be curious and make sure it wasn't for anything bad," Liam explained.

"Man, what is it with you and trying to defend everyone except me?" Chaz begrudgingly told him.

"I'm just giving options, not defending anyone in particular," Liam answered. Chaz shook his head with a look of disappointment.

"Whatever," Chaz said as he walked away. Liam then continued with his work. At any moment, he was expecting someone else to go up to him and complain about something else, but much to his gratitude, no one did. So when the time came to leave work, he was one of the last to punch out and get inside his car. It was a little after eight at night. He knew exactly what Josh and Mike would be doing, but he wasn't too sure what he would be up to. It was far too early for him to go back home. He needed to keep his mind occupied somehow.

He drove back home. As soon as he entered the house, he rushed to the bathroom and turned the shower water on to the hottest setting. He walked over to the sink and noticed the crack still there. He rolled his eyes, remembering he was getting close to having to buy another one. He jumped into the shower and managed to waste another half hour.

By the time he had gotten out of the shower and fully dressed, it was a couple of minutes past nine-thirty. He returned to his car and decided that he would be eating out in a restaurant by himself. He drove to his destination and found a parking spot close to the entrance. He paused in his car for a few minutes. His hands remained on the steering wheel as he looked directly at it.

'LINDA! LINDA!'

He heard a panicky voice in his mind screaming out, looking for someone lost among all the debris. He shook his head and then turned up the volume of his radio so that the music was louder than his thoughts. It was still the same slow-paced and relaxing music that he always played. He hadn't quite learned how to fully overcome his mind, but he had learned ways to calm it down, soothe it, and buy him some extra time.

The name Linda was no longer loud in his head. It was now a faint sound in the background of the music itself. He turned off the engine, and the music quickly went away. He opened the door, allowing himself to feel the cold. It would distract his mind during the walk to the restaurant. He walked at an average pace and held the door for a couple walking inside. He nodded with a simplistic smile and then walked in as they thanked him.

He was met by the host after the couple had been sat in a booth. The host looked at Liam and then down to the seating charts. There was a moment of silence; Liam felt the host was waiting for someone to join him.

"A table for one, please," Liam casually spoke.

"Table for one? Alrighty, would you prefer a regular table, maybe a bar seat? Or on a booth?" The host asked him calmly.

"Anything except the bar," Liam quickly replied. The host nodded, wrote something down on the paper, and then looked up at Liam again.

"Alright, follow me, please," he said. Liam obliged and followed the host over to a booth seat.

"The waitress will be right with you. If you have any questions feel free to ask, my name is Pablo," the host told him with a gentle and caring smile as he placed the menu on top of the table.

"Thank you," Liam answered while forcing a smile. He grabbed the menu and began looking through it carefully. He read the description of any meal that caught his attention. It only took a few moments before a young woman appeared at his table, most likely a college student.

"Hello, my name is Shila, and I am going to be your waitress for the night. Can I start you off with anything to drink?" She asked with high levels of energy and confidence. She sounded like someone carefree and bubbly.

"Umm, I'll start with water," he replied.

"A water, alright. Would you like any appetizers? Do you need more time to look over the menu?" She pleasantly asked.

"I'm going to skip the appetizer. I do need a few more minutes," he told her.

"No problem! I'll go grab you that water and be right back," she told him. She walked out of sight, leaving Liam to look through the menu. The decision was becoming more difficult than he had anticipated. He managed to pick up his food once Shila returned with his water. He didn't have to wait long for his food to be ready. The restaurant was pretty dead and probably had something to do with it.

He ate his food slowly, and once he finished, he ended up leaving a thirty percent tip before taking off and heading back to his house. Once he was home, he took a seat on his couch. He looked to his right and noticed that he still hadn't moved his journal. He started reaching for it but then changed his mind. He returned to the bathroom, turning on the sink, never looking at the mirror. He splashed some hot water on his face as the screams for Linda began returning to his mind. Finally, he sighed and left the bathroom.

Nothing much changed throughout the week. People complaining about someone, more screams and taunting on his mind, and finding ways to get through each day. Until the day came, another Wednesday, for once, he was able to wake up with a sense of optimism.

Chapter 4

Stefanie gently opened the door for Liam. He walked in with a half-smile. He had been excited about this the entire week, yet he still felt anxious and nervous. Like the week before, Stefanie was dressed casually in jeans and a simple cardigan. She wasn't trying to make herself seem fancy, she wasn't trying to impress, she was being comfortable, focusing on helping. Again, like the week before, Liam sat in the middle of the couch and hunched down a little. Stefanie took a seat before him, holding the same notepad she had during their first session. Liam wondered if she had a different pad for every client or if she used the same for all of them.

"Tell me about your week," she said gently. It was an interesting start to the session, but it did the trick.

"It was, like, pretty much every single other week. Annoying coworkers, a cracked sink, too much noise in my head," Liam responded quickly.

"Interesting, it seems like quite a bit. Tell me about those annoying coworkers," she asked as she jotted down a few notes on the notepad. Liam was intrigued, he had mentioned various things, stuff that probably sounded a bit bizarre, such as a cracked sink and noise in his head, yet she went straight for the annoying coworkers, something that he was sure the majority of the people would complain about.

"A few people just like to talk about this person or that person. Always negative, one of them invited me out last Thursday after work to go to a bar with him and his friend."

"Did you go?" She asked curiously as she listened carefully.

"I declined."

"How come?"

"He is pretty douchey, but I don't quite trust myself being around people in general," he answered honestly.

"Is there a reason why you do not trust being around people?" Stefanie asked as she continued to eye him with a gentle smile. He breathed in some air before he began answering.

"I'm afraid of what I could accidentally do. I mean, think about it, in the last few months, I've had to buy a couple of sinks for the bathroom already. Now I have another one I cracked last week," he explained.

"That explains your mention of a cracked sink. I was going to get to that at some point," she answered with a smile.

"Wow, you got me there without even asking me," he responded, lost for words.

"I had no idea that's how it was going to happen, but things just happen in life in ways we sometimes don't expect," she told him. Then, before returning to him, she wrote down a few more notes on her notepad.

"I am surprised, though," Liam said slowly.

"Surprised?" Stefanie asked curiously.

"How you haven't been bombarding me with questions about the time when I was... umm... Faceless... and my powers," Liam said.

"Well, do I have some curiosities? Sure, but I am not here to satisfy my curiosities; I am here to help you. This is about you. This place is your haven for talking openly about anything," Stefanie responded. Before Liam had a chance to speak, she continued.

"I also noticed how you sort of hesitated on the name Faceless."

"I never cared for that name," he responded honestly.

"Any particular reason as to why?"

"I didn't choose that name. It was given to me by social media, and then it basically stuck around. It was a name given because I wore a blank silver mask with no eyes cut through. You know when you read comic books and watch superhero movies. There are always costumes for the superheroes as well as the villains? The villains always have their villain names as well. So it makes sense that the superheroes have their costumes. I did it to hide my identity, which worked very well. However, out of the six supervillains I faced, only two had their own costume and a villain name. All the others just simply used their real name."

"That is an interesting point you make. But, I'd like to step back and return to the people at work. Have you ever tried spending time with any of them outside of work? Is there anyone in there that you can get along with?"

"There is Henry and Tati. They're outcasts in there. She has sort of this goth and punk mix look. With his dyed hair, Henry has a bit of the punk thing going. But, unfortunately, I work with too many judgmental people, minus these two."

"Have they invited you to hang out with them?" Stefanie asked as she wrote down a few more notes. Liam carefully eyed it but never questioned what exactly she was writing.

"They did, the same day as Josh did. I also declined. The more so because I don't want to accidentally do something dumb."

"What makes you think you would end up doing something dumb?" Stefanie questioned him.

"I don't know, the broken sinks?" Liam responded, a little puzzled.

"How long have you worked where you are?" She casually asked him.

"Like a year or so."

"Has there been any sort of incidents that have happened there?" She asked. Liam was trying to figure out where she was going with the question.

"Not yet, no."

"It seems like a year is a fairly long time when putting it into perspective. Is it fair to say that perhaps we can reframe some of your thoughts?" Stefanie asked him. Liam was thinking about it for a second. Then, he remembered her mentioning something about reframing the previous week.

"I'm not sure what you mean," Liam admitted.

"Well, when you start having thoughts about something, let's say negative and discouraging thoughts, you can reframe them into something more positive. For example, I do not want to go out because I am afraid I will do something terrible. Still, I have worked for a year around people, and nothing bad has happened, so it will be fine," Stefanie explained to him. Liam was frozen for a few moments and then leaned back on the couch.

"Huh," was all he managed to say while he started thinking. Stefanie was watching him with a smile. This was good; it was making him think. Even if it wasn't going to be an immediate change, he would at least now have that imprinted in his mind. Perhaps he would even be able to start applying it when he could. While the idea seemed so simple, she has had her fair share of clients telling her how life-changing the concept of reframing thoughts had become for them. So many people did not seem to think about that until it was brought up to them. She gave Liam a few more moments before she went back into talking.

"Alright, let's talk about that noise in your head now," she started as she observed his reaction. She could tell that this particular topic was a little tougher on him when he sighed.

"I... I... it's just noise," he finally responded, stumbling over his words. She found it interesting how suddenly he could barely speak. She noted something and then turned back to him.

"Alright, let's pause that for a moment. Then, perhaps we can start reviewing what you want to take from this therapy. Different people choose to come to therapy for different reasons. Some because they want to make their love life better. Others because of work, so there is no wrong answer for this," Stefanie told him. She was beginning to understand why he was there and what he probably wanted. But as the saying goes, she wanted to hear straight from the horse's mouth.

"I... I want to... I want to be able to sleep... I want the noise in my head to go away... I want to sort of live a normal life... if not fully normal, then at least a little bit," he responded while holding back tears.

"That is all fair, and there is no reason why you shouldn't want that. No reason why we can't work on that," Stefanie gently told him.

"I'm going, to be honest with you. I am skeptical; I don't think it's possible. I don't think we can get there. I don't mean it personally either," Liam told her.

"I'm not taking it personally. Everything you are feeling is perfectly acceptable. It's not easy. It could take a lot of time. But I promise I will be here to do the best I can to help, and I think you're stronger than you realize. I'm obviously not talking about physically, but mentally," she responded to him.

"I do like this. Honestly, even though getting through every week is always extremely shitty, this week was a tiny bit better because I was looking forward to being here," Liam admitted to her.

"Have you ever talked to anyone about who you were and everything that you are going through?" Stefanie asked him.

"No. You are the only person in this world that knows my real identity," Liam admitted.

"There you go. The fact that you get to talk about it and just let yourself loose may be why you look forward to being here," Stefanie told him. Liam agreed. It was undoubtedly helping him. But, whether it was her job or not, she didn't act like it was.

"Besides work, how else did you spend your week?" Stefanie asked him. Liam started to rub a little bit on the couch. It felt nice and smooth and was very comfortable to sit at. He then scratched his neck and noticed a pile of planners on a stand next to Stefanie. He gazed around the room again. Like last time, it was still dimly lit. Stefanie patiently remained in her seat as she crossed one leg over the other. Finally, Liam stood up and walked toward one of the paintings on the wall.

"Caught your interest?" Stefanie asked.

"It's an actual painting of scenery. I'm surprised you don't have the things you see on movies and shows."

"What things?" She asked curiously.

"You know, wave it in my face and ask what I see. Some people might see a butterfly; others might see a face," Liam answered. Stefanie started laughing.

"Maybe I have some in my bag, and I haven't pulled them out just yet," she joked with him. Liam smiled, it was his first in the session, and Stefanie felt a little victory there. He looked back at the painting. It was an interesting one. It was a beach full of people staring at a boat far in the distance. However, one particular individual seemed to be discretely focused on. The coloring appeared the same as every other person's. Still, somehow Liam felt something had been done that brought greater focus to that specific person. This person was staring toward the boat like everyone else, but his posture seemed different somehow. He couldn't figure it out.

He turned to look at the next painting. This one was more straightforward; it was two silhouettes holding hands in the middle of a stadium. The rest of the crowd were not silhouettes, but they all pointed angrily toward the two holding hands.

"Interesting," Liam mentioned.

"What's interesting?" Stefanie asked, curious to hear his intake of the painting.

"They're silhouettes; we can't see who they are. Yet everyone is pointing at them, angry as if judging them."

"Interesting take. Sometimes it doesn't matter what we do. People are still going to judge. Sometimes you don't have to do anything, and you will still be judged. If you look deeper into the crowd, you can see that some have hand-shaped hearts in the direction of the silhouettes. While others are pointing angrily at other people in the crowd," Stefanie alerted him. Sure enough, he started to find those people. Maybe the painting wasn't as straightforward as he had initially thought.

"Even the paintings have psychological lessons," he spoke as he

34

turned around and returned to the couch.

"Do people ever lay down on the couch as we see in the movies?" Liam asked.

"Some people choose to lay down. Most of my clients just sit, though," Stefanie responded.

"Let's talk about your sleep, something that you've mentioned that you struggle with," she started. Liam stroked his beard, which still hadn't been taken care of. The bags on his eyes were still just as bad as the previous week.

"Well, my mind... it just runs wild. I can't seem to shut it off. I've tried everything, well maybe I haven't tried an actual tranquilizer yet," he joked. Stefanie wrote down a few more things before turning back to him.

"Maybe, small steps. Perhaps start doing some things differently and see if you feel refreshed."

"Like what things?" Liam quickly asked, as his right foot anxiously tapped on the floor.

"That will have to be up to you. Some people go and get a haircut to feel like a new person. Someone else might go try a new hobby they always wanted to try. The possibilities are endless; they end up being related to your life. Sometimes your mind just needs a bit of a change rather than the same thing over and over," she eloquently explained to him.

"Hmm. I'll have to think about it," Liam responded as he rubbed his beard.

"Alright, then you'll think about perhaps doing something different, even if it's something small," Stefanie told him. Liam nodded slowly. He was in thought for a little bit. Stefanie remained in silence, giving him the opportunity. Then, after a few moments, she finally spoke.

"So you have been at your job for roughly a year, you say. You load trucks up. You mentioned earlier that some of those coworkers are always complaining about one another; how does that make you feel?" Liam moved his back against the couch as he took a deep breath. Stefanie watched him intently. She was trying to read his facial expressions. She was, however, having a difficult time doing so.

"I don't know how I feel, honestly," he told her. He looked around the room, his teeth showing as he started thinking. She gave him the time to do so. Although the remaining time in the session was running lower, she did not like to rush her clients.

"Part of me feels as if it is fine because it distracts me from my thoughts. But," he continued as he let out a couple of breaths.

"Meanwhile, you also don't quite enjoy all the negativity, I take it?" Stefanie added with a smile. Liam nodded as his eyes opened up wide. It wasn't out of annoyance. It was out of surprise.

"Yeah, exactly that," he admitted. Stefanie smiled as she placed the notepad on top of her planners on a little counter beside her. She continued with her gentle smile and put her hands together as she hunched forward on her chair.

"Perhaps that could be a lesson and solution taken from that context," she told him.

"How so?"

"Maybe, it's not exactly what they are saying that is keeping your mind occupied and silencing it. Perhaps it's the fact that people are talking to you about something else. I am deducing from that, and I could be wrong. Of course, it is not something I can say is factual. Still, I deduce that maybe if they were talking to you about a delicious meal, or something good, it would still have the same effect of silencing your mind," Stefanie carefully explained to him. Liam raised one eyebrow. He had once again become speechless.

"Maybe what you need is to just be with different people. Maybe deciding to spend more time with Henry and Tati might help," Stefanie suggested.

"I just... I just don't know. I don't think I'm ready to just go out and be in big groups of people outside of work," Liam answered.

"You don't have to be out with big groups of people, you could just spend more time with them at work, or you could invite the two of them over to your house and have some sort of game night or just a social night," Stefanie suggested. Liam was thinking. The idea was making him uncomfortable at the current point, but he knew that Stefanie was making a good point. He turned to her and forced another smile.

"I'll think about it," he told her. She returned the smile and leaned back against her chair again.

"That's something, at least. So, what will be your goals for this upcoming week?" Stefanie asked him.

"Goals?" He asked, confused.

"Yeah, set some goals so we can talk about it when you come here next week. It can be one thing. It could be minimal, just something to get you going."

"Umm, I guess that... I'll work on finding something to do differently than I've been doing?"

"Alright. We can go with that. If, for some reason, you are not able to accomplish it, don't feel bad. It happens, and it takes time. For next week, do you want the same day and time? Does that work?" Stefanie asked him. There was a bit of a disappointment for Liam with those words. It meant that their session was almost over, and he would have to wait another week to come back and talk. The sessions felt so great and so short as well. He understood that he wasn't the center of the universe, and she had other clients to help too.

"Yeah, that works for me," he told her. She grabbed one of her planners and flipped a few pages before writing something down on one of them. Finally, she closed the planner and placed it on the notepad.

"Great! Before you go, do you have questions or any possible concerns? Are you going to be alright for the week?" Stefanie gently asked him. He nodded his head. This time she was capable of reading his facial expression. He felt sad, and down that he had to go.

"Yeah, I'll be alright. I don't have any current questions," he responded as he stood up from the couch and started heading toward the door. She stood up and started heading towards the door to open it for him, but he beat her to it himself. So instead, he turned towards her and forced a weak smile.

"Thank you, have a goodnight."

"You as well," she answered. He walked outside the room and closed the door behind him. He glanced at the door and exited the building, ready to return to reality.

Chapter 5

There was a sound of keys right outside the house. The door swung open, and Stefanie almost looked like a shadow with the lights off as she walked inside her home. Then, finally, she spoke something out loud, and the lights came on automatically. She grabbed her work cell phone and placed it beside her keys on a counter near the door.

She had bought the house about a year prior and was quite proud of her achievement. It took a bit of restraint to save enough for a down payment, but it was worth it. She could call this her home, even though it wasn't that big of a house. That was alright, though, she didn't expect this to be her forever home, but it was the start for her. A time would come when she could upgrade to a bigger house of her own accord. This one did not have a second floor or an addict. It had an unfinished basement that she only cared for a little besides storage and washing and drying machines. The house had one bathroom, two bedrooms, and a living room. There was a small backyard in the back where she had put a round table with a comfortable seat.

During the warmer weather, she often went outside with her laptop and did some work. She had turned the second bedroom into an office. If any client elected for video chat, that's where she would go. During the colder weather, she would go there instead of the outdoors to do any work she needed on the laptop. It helped eliminate distractions around her house; she had few. She kept things simple and minimal, but the television was always her biggest distraction.

She walked over to the kitchen; it was well-organized and maintained. It was mostly clean, except for her stove, which was a bit greasy. She knew she needed to clean it, but either she had no time some days, or on the days that she did have some time, she just didn't feel like spending them cleaning a stove. So she only had a few visitors to worry about. She opened the refrigerator, which was quite full. She searched for a while and decided on a water bottle. She closed the door and turned away while opening her bottle and drinking from it.

It was starting to get late; it was already past nine. Generally, she would lie on the couch to relax for a few minutes while watching television and then head to bed. This night, however, she decided she would do some extra work. She walked towards her bedroom office and opened the door. She turned the light on, sat by her desk, and opened the laptop. She grabbed one of her empty notepads from under the desk and put it beside her laptop, with a pen on top.

She wanted to try and find out anything she possibly could on Faceless. She was getting to know the man behind the mask in person, but what was his history like while he was Faceless? She knew she wouldn't find anything correlated to the man named Liam Lewis; after all, she was the only person who knew that Liam and Faceless were the same people. She could, if she wanted, look for any possible social media that Liam would have, though she doubted he would have any. Besides, she didn't want to start going that route. She wanted to simply learn more about the history of Faceless.

She opened up her search engine site and then played with her fingers, trying to figure out what she wanted to search for. The room she was in was pretty cozy. She had made sure the heat was on at just the right temperature. The walls themselves had some artwork on them. Some appeared to be just regular drawings of sceneries, while others seemed to have some bizarre and unusual shapes to them. The curtain on the window was a light color and pushed aside to allow visuals of the backyard. The window itself was closed, but the blinds were up as well. The light in the room was dimly lit, much like the room she worked in.

She began typing in the search bar, 'Faceless First Appearance,' and then hit enter. The screen loaded quickly, and plenty of results showed up. Some headlines were bizarre, such as, 'Alien lands On Earth, masquerades as a superhero.' Followed by another related headline, 'Where did Faceless hide his UFO?' Stefanie shook her head while rolling her eyes. So many conspiracy theories. She felt one of them would be close to the truth somewhere along the line, considering what Liam had already told her.

She found a legitimate report about the first time Faceless had made public appearances. It was roughly two months after Jack McDay had first showed up. Jack McDay, of course, was the first known supervillain, most likely the one Liam had followed. There was a link that directed her to a profile of Jack. The man had a reasonably decent position in a medical facility. Still, after abusing his access power, he was fired. He was blacklisted from ever working in any medical facility. It wasn't long afterward that he lost his marriage, his car, and his house. Eventually, he disappeared until he resurfaced again, destroying public

39

vehicles and businesses with superpowers.

Eventually, he was confronted by Faceless, and the two battled it out in the central city, where more buildings were destroyed. This time though, there had been some casualties. They sent Jack to jail, but it didn't take long for him to escape and start causing destruction once again. This time he was furious and started attacking random innocent homes. He was once again confronted by Faceless and ended up being killed in the ensuing battle.

Stefanie was so focused on reading the article that she jumped up from her seat the moment her personal cell phone began to ring. She quickly glanced at the screen, and the moment she saw the name on it, she grabbed the cell phone with her left hand while she continued to scroll down with her right. The next thing in the article was pictures of both battles between Jack and Faceless.

"Hey, mom, how are you?" She answered the phone.

"I'm doing alright, sweety. Sorry for calling you so late; I just... I just was feeling a little sad and down. Every time I hear your voice, I feel so much better," her mother answered from the other end of the line.

"It's alright, mom, you're never a bother by calling. I'd rather you call than feel sad," Stefanie responded as she leaned back on her chair and paused her search. She rolled the chair in a circle like a little kid.

"Ever since your father passed away last year, it's been tough. I hadn't lived alone since before you were even born. So you can imagine it's been over twenty-eight years."

"That's understandable, mom."

"Hey, at least I still remember your age! I still have my memory intact," her mother joked. Stefanie let out a little laugh with teary eyes.

"Are things generally good though with you?" Stefanie asked.

"Oh yes, I have terrific, friendly neighbors. People are always willing to help me over here. So what are you doing this late at night?"

"It's not overly late, just a bit past ten, mom. I am just doing some research."

"Work-related, I am guessing?"

"Yes, it is."

"Anything exciting?" Her mother asked.

"You know I can't talk about that, mom..." Stefanie paused momentarily, wondering if she had just offended her mother.

"I'm sorry, mother, I didn't mean it in a bad way. It is not that I do not trust you. It's just that I take this job seriously and signed privacy papers for each client."

"Oh, honey, I am not offended. On the contrary, I am so proud of you for taking your job seriously. Ever since you were a kid, you have always wanted to help people one way or another. You were always very good at saying the right things, even to me," her mom answered. Stefanie couldn't see her mother at the moment, but she imagined the soft and kind smile that her mother always gave her.

"Thanks, mom," Stefanie managed to say, her eyes wetter.

"I'm sure all your clients love and appreciate you," her mom encouraged her.

"I hope so. They are all so different from one another, coming to see me for various reasons. Some just need someone to talk to, others to heal, and others to somehow repair themselves. Still, the one thing they all have in common is that they are all good people and want to be better," Stefanie told her.

"I know you'll get them there, honey. I think I will let you go for the night. I am thrilled I got to hear your voice. You are still coming this summer to see me, right?" Her mom gently asked.

"Of course, I'll be taking a vacation sometime in the summer, so I can go see you."

"I'll be looking forward to it. Have you started seeing anyone?" Her mother casually asked. Stefanie laughed a little.

"No, I have not, mom."

"That's ok. As long as you are doing what you love and being happy with yourself, that's all that matters. But honey, I think you should get a dog." Stefanie started laughing as she wiped away tears that she was glad her mom couldn't see.

"I've been thinking about it, mom; maybe soon."

"Good. Anyways honey, goodnight."

"Goodnight, mom," Stefanie responded as she heard the other end of the line hang up. Stefanie covered her face with both hands as she cried for a bit. Her father had passed away roughly a year prior, and her mother had lived independently since then. Stefanie had offered her mom to go up there as long as she needed to keep her company. It wasn't that she didn't trust that her mother could take care of herself. It was the fact that her mother had lived with the company for so long that adjusting to being alone every day could have been a rough start.

Her mother had insisted she stay where she was, as she followed her dream and was happy. Around the same time, she had closed on her new home. Stefanie was quite proud of her mother. She had been doing well on her own. There were nights like these when her mother would simply call her to hear her voice, even if they talked about the same things they had in the past.

Her father had been a good father and husband. This was even more reason why it pained Stefanie to find out that some people didn't have that same luxury. The world could be sad, but she knew from her job that it also had a lot of people wanting to do better, people with good hearts. She witnessed some of these people in their most vulnerable states, yet they still managed to keep going.

She wiped the tears from her face and then returned to her laptop, where she had left a few pictures of Faceless against his first villain. She decided to simply type Faceless on her search engine. There were a few sites that popped up for cosplay costumes. She scrolled down, skipping each of those sites. There was even one exclusively for fanfiction on Faceless. She then came across videos. Some were from people who had recorded moments with their cell phones, others were simply fan-made videos, and others were documentaries. She clicked on one of the shorter videos.

It began playing, and the person filming it appeared to be hiding under a car. The footage was difficult to see, covered mainly by asphalt concrete. There was a pair of feet walking in the direction of another couple of feet. Stefanie could hear the heavy breathing of someone else right next to the person filming.

"Shhh," the person filming was heard saying. He tried to stick the cell phone out a bit. It appeared that the two people were having a dialogue. Still, it was pretty inaudible with all the screaming and sounds of loud car engines.

"They're going to fight again, they're going to fight again," whispered a man that sounded to be in his early twenties.

"We should get out of here then... What if one of them gets sent flying toward this car!" The voice of a woman answered a little louder than his.

"Shh... We'll be fine; if we get out of here, they'll see us!" The man said just as the two feet started running toward each other, and then there was a loud crashing noise, and one of them was sent flying sideways.

"Oh shit! Did you see that? DID YOU SEE THAT?" The young man said a little too loud. Stefanie could not tell if it was excitement, adrenaline, or fear. Or perhaps it was all three of them. The video ended shortly after that. She continued to scroll through and found many similar videos to the first one. Another one she saw, people had been recording from inside of their job, others from their houses. There had even been those less discreet and filmed from the middle of the street.

She then decided that she would watch one that was more in the style of a documentary. Considering it wasn't officially made, she would be careful about how she would take the information in. Somewhere along the line, there were bound to be discrepancies, but maybe, just maybe, it could still help her understand her client better. And she may be able to help him.

Chapter 6

He was looking straight ahead at a man with a smug grin. The man's face was full of dust, and his hair was all over the place. The man's tuxedo had rips everywhere, and the white shirt had plenty of blood spots from cuts he had received. Behind the man, smoke was coming from a car on fire. Liam looked back to see the house that he was protecting. He looked forward again, his eyes fixated on the grinning man ahead.

"How about we stop playtime?" The man spoke with sternness. The man dashed forward with incredible speed. Liam's eyes looked down just in time to witness the man's palm hit him in the chest. He felt himself being dragged back by nothing but the force that had been put through his chest. His feet lifted off the ground, and everything felt like a big slow-motion moment. He continued to fly backwards, his arms extended out, unable to do anything. Then he felt a sharp on his back, and the next thing he knew, he was going through the brick that made the house, on the exact spot where the window had been. He looked to his right and saw glass floating right by his face. He then looked left to see the same thing. He still felt as if everything was in slow motion.

Then, everything started to feel like it all sped up. He kept flying backwards; what initially had appeared to be a simple palm to the chest had been something much more powerful. Then, finally, he went through the wall on the other side and stopped once he hit a tree. Even his bulletproof skin had felt that maybe bullets couldn't kill him, but whatever force had hit him was strong enough to overpower the skin shield he had. He shook his head, trying to compose himself; all he could hear in his ears was a big buzz. It sounded like people were screaming back inside the house, but he couldn't tell.

It took him a few minutes to get back up, and once he did, he rushed right back inside the house. Miraculously his mask had remained on despite some of his costume being ripped. Once inside the house, he noticed a man on the ground with glass sticking from his clothes while blood dripped on the floor as he rocked himself back and forth in pain. Then, closer to the back of the house, where he had flown through to the backyard, he saw a woman lying on the ground motionless.

He quickly checked her pulse, panicking and hoping she was alive. He felt a slight pulse but then noticed something horrifying. Her legs appeared to have been twisted in the commotion, something he wasn't entirely sure could be healed.

"Oh god, oh no! What have I done?" He said to himself as he began to cry behind his mask. It was then that he heard a voice coming from the outside.

"You ready to come out here and get beat up some more? Or should I take care of it inside the house for you?" He heard the voice. Liam knew he needed to compose himself, this was a horrifying sight, but his enemy was still out there and extremely dangerous. If he didn't handle the situation, many more people would lose their homes, become permanently injured, and even die. It was then that he decided to fly outside. He ascended up high quite a few feet, hoping the enemy would take the bait and follow him.

He looked down, waiting for his enemy to fly up so that he could then lead him away elsewhere, perhaps somewhere without people. But instead, the man looked up at him with the most menacing smirk yet. After that, Liam noticed people hiding in all kinds of places; some had phones out, and others were hiding their faces in fear. Just then, the villain dashed inside the house, and what followed was painful screaming coming from within.

His eyes quickly opened, and he lifted himself up. He started breathing heavily, feeling the chills. This had been the same dream he had the previous night. It was a battle he had with one of his adversaries. It had lasted far too long, and many bad things had happened. He grabbed his comforter and wrapped it around him, shaking, sweating, with every breath feeling like a full-time job. He looked at his clock; he had slept less than two hours. It didn't surprise him.

The image of the man with the smirk returned to his mind. Tanner Brown had been the second supervillain he had ever encountered. He had been far more dangerous and deranged than Jack himself. Jack went on a rampage at first, purely out of anger. The second time was out of anger again, but more with a vengeance in mind for being caught. Tanner, on the other hand, enjoyed seeing the destruction and people suffering. He had always been psychotic, which was why scientists picked him. They used him to see if the serum would affect different personalities differently.

Liam's shaking began to calm down, his breathing a little more relaxed. He tried to take his mind away from Tanner. But, unfortunately, it wouldn't do him any good to think about the worst of the worst. Liam looked at the time; it was nearly seven in the morning, a little less than two hours of sleep this time. He rolled his eyes in frustration. It had been two days since he had seen Stefanie, and his sleep hadn't improved yet. No fault of Stefanie's; he hadn't done anything towards his goal yet, but he wasn't overly concerned. He still had another five days to figure out what he could do.

He stood up from the bed and began walking towards the kitchen. He grabbed a glass, filled it with water, and quickly drank it. His eyes started hurting from the lack of sleep, and the bags under them were worse than ever. He walked over to his couch and took a seat. The journal was still in the same spot since he had thrown it.

He sighed and then connected his phone to one of the speakers in the room and put on some relaxing music. He was off, so he didn't have to think about heading to work. He closed his eyes, hoping a different location with music would help him fall asleep. It didn't help. His mind kept going from one thought to the next.

Fuck off, mind.

No, you fuck off. You're the one thinking about that stupid sink for no reason.

Actually, no, I was not. I was thinking about wanting to sleep.

Yeah, yeah, you still have a crack in that sink. Plus, you're talking to yourself in your head again. You oughta just lock yourself up in a loony institution right away!

Anyways. The sink, I should start finding the cheapest sink if I'm going to keep spending money on it.

Oh, shit, remember when I first met Tati? She did warn me that a bunch of jerks worked there.

Ah, wait, shoot, I get paid this week, right? Oh wow, I just remembered I need to buy groceries!

His mind just kept going and going. Somehow he managed to get to thinking about the time of dinosaurs. That's when he realized he wouldn't be falling asleep anytime soon. He stood up and headed outside. Rather than going to his car, he started walking around the block. Perhaps a walk could help soothe his mind down. He looked around and started watching as some people left their homes to go to work while others brought their kids to the school bus.

Look at all these lucky people you didn't kill, unlike other unlucky ones.

I didn't kill anyone!

Well, maybe not intentionally, but you were in those battles with those super-powered bad people. Had you not engaged them, those people would still be alive!

Many others, more people would have been dead.

Is that what you tell yourself to make yourself feel better? Sure thing, sure thing.

Liam started shaking his head quickly. He wanted to begin slapping himself, turning his mind off if he could, but he knew it would invite too much attention. Something he didn't want at the moment. Liam's conversations with himself inside his mind were becoming worse. He wondered if it was something he should mention to Stefanie the next time he was there? Would she confirm his suspicions that he should be locked away somewhere? The conversations didn't even make sense. Why did he refer to himself as if he was someone else? He asked too many questions, making him turn around and return to his house.

Nothing was helping him. It was going to be one of those days. Once in front of the house, he made a last-minute decision to get inside his car and drive away. He needed to do something. The walk wasn't helping him, and staying inside the house would not help him either. Perhaps it was time to do some grocery shopping. He guessed that it would keep him occupied for an hour or so. At least, that's what he hoped. He would figure out the remainder of the day afterward.

Inside the store, he stood in front of a section of pasta. He stared at it with his hands holding onto the carriage. Even choosing which pasta he wanted was proving to be stressful. There were three boxes of the same exact pasta but three different brands. The price was the other difference, one being a nickel cheaper.

Why can't they just have one? Why do they need different brands... Wait...

Liam then noticed two more brands of the same pasta. Frustrated, he decided to close his eyes and simply grab one. In the process, he knocked a few other boxes to the floor.

"Shit," he accidentally spoke out. Realizing he had said it aloud, he searched to ensure no one had overheard him. He picked up the boxes and placed them back on the shelves. Why did everything else seem to follow every time one thing went wrong? Still frustrated, Liam left the aisle and finished his shopping.

He had gone shopping to keep his mind distracted, yet somehow he left feeling even more annoyed than before. He opened the back seat of his car and placed his groceries inside, and then jumped into the driver's seat. He looked at his cell phone really quick, looking at the time. He then threw the phone onto the passenger's seat. The phone hit the seat and then fell to the floor.

"Piece of shit," he murmured. He started the engine and then began looking at the steering wheel.

The people, the house, Tanner. Not my fault... I couldn't control him... No, you provoked him, you did it. Had you not... Had you not tried to outwit him, those people would have been alive. It is all your fault, even if everyone pointed fingers at Tanner. They had to; they had no choice. They couldn't vilify their hero.

Liam closed his hands into fists and then was about to smack the steering wheel but stopped himself just in time. Considering what he had done to a few sinks in the bathroom already, he would end up destroying the steering wheel. He took a couple of deep breaths.

If you feel so guilty, so responsible, why not turn yourself in to the police?

They never made a substantial effort to even catch me, to begin with. They wanted me around. Plus, I could be far more dangerous if I was in prison. A closed space provoked and poked a lot more. More people would end up getting hurt or worse. At least, at least I can control myself out here far better.

Liam backed out of his car and left the parking lot. He started heading back towards his house, where his mind kept returning to Tanner. No matter how much he tried to get him out of his mind, he just kept returning. Even in death, he still had to see and hear Tanner. This must be part of his punishment.

He had once been a kid fascinated with superhero movies and comic books. None of which had ever prepared him for how dire and torturous it truly was. In the stories, the superhero would always win without causing severe casualties. Destruction was the worst of it. It was all a lie. In reality, destruction was the best; there was so much worse. None of the movies or comics told the story of reality. Silliness was all it was.

Once Liam returned home and put his groceries away, he returned to the bathroom. Not once did he glance at the mirror. Instead, Liam splashed his face with hot water again, and just when he was about to grab hold of the sink, he walked out of the bathroom and into his room. He slammed the door shut, cracking it near the handle, and then dove into bed with his face down. He placed his head between the pillows and started screaming into them. The pillows did a better job than he had anticipated absorbing much of the sound. He then turned around, breathing heavily as he began to cry.

His loud sobbing echoed across the room as he looked up at the ceiling. He felt miserable, useless, worthless, and like a gigantic fraud. He had always wanted to be a good person when he was a kid, a teenager, and even as a young adult. Instead, he had turned out to be the biggest fraud. In his mind, he felt like a coward, unable to cope with his actions and decisions. He wanted nothing more than not to blame himself, yet he could not find any reason not to.

He barely kept in touch with both of his parents. Neither had ever done anything wrong and had always cared for him. He regretted the day he had decided to follow Jack back to the lab. He should have allowed the authorities to do their job. Sooner or later, someone was bound to catch him, right? Why was the world so complicated?

He would remain there for the rest of the day, frozen and looking at the ceiling. He wasn't sleeping, but he wasn't in reality either. He had created an imaginary place in his mind in some way to attempt to cope with his unbearable truth. The hours passed, and the day came to an end. Once again, it was too late when he finally fell asleep.

The week continued to pass, and with each day that ended, he still had not accomplished the goal he had set in therapy. It was true that Stefanie had told him not to worry about it if he couldn't make it, but that was not the answer he wanted to give. Time was running out, and he would have to think of something. It didn't have to be drastic; it didn't have to be outlandish. Even something small would work, at least according to Stefanie.

At work, Josh wasn't really speaking to him. Liam guessed the man was still offended over him not going out the previous week. Liam wasn't too concerned about it. At least Henry and Tati still spoke to him the same as they always had. He was glad too. It was a week he really needed their more positive energy around. The days passed normally, and then Wednesday came.

He still had yet to achieve any goal. He'd not gotten out of his comfort zone and done anything differently. He started pacing around his kitchen anxiously as he stroked his beard. He needed to think of something before his appointment later in the day. He didn't want to go in there and deliver the news of failure. He wanted to walk into Stefanie's office proudly that he had taken the first step. He needed to trust her. She had chosen that job because she wanted to help people get better. She would lead him right.

The kitchen wasn't helping him think, so he changed to the living room. Maybe in this particular room, he would come up with a solution. He sat on the couch, laid back, and lifted his head. A spider was crawling through the ceiling. His first instinct was to get rid of it, but then he realized it didn't matter. The spider was doing him no harm. Perhaps the two of them could co-exist peacefully.

"If you drop on me, we will have a problem," he warned the spider. He then put both hands on his face and rubbed his beard. In a manner of seconds, he jumped up from his couch. His eyes lit up as if he'd just seen a treasure filled with gold. He nodded at the wall across from him and gave it a thumbs up.

"I got it! I know what I have to do," he told the wall. He left the living room and grabbed his car keys and wallet before leaving.

Chapter 7

Stefanie was on her seat writing down a few things from her previous client. It was then that there was a soft knock on the door. She stood up and casually walked towards the door and opened it. Then, puzzled, she stared at the person standing before her.

"I am sorry, but I'm expecting a client already. You can go online and put all of your info, then when I get the chance, I'll call you back, and we can set up an appointment," Stefanie told the man. The man was quite handsome, and his face was clean-shaven while his hair was short and combed to the side. He had a soft smirk on his face and remained quiet. After moments, Stefanie recognized the man's green eyes and the bags under them.

"Liam? Wow! You look so different!" she told him with a big smile. Then, she motioned for him to walk inside, which he did.

"I almost failed the goal we had set, but I realized earlier today that shaving and getting my hair done might be a good change for me," Liam admitted to her.

"Absolutely. Sometimes changing our looks a bit can help enhance our confidence. Enhancing confidence can lead to many new things, like pushing yourself out of your comfort zone a little more," she explained to Liam. He sat on the couch as he'd done the previous two weeks.

"Yeah, I'm not entirely sure what it looks like, though," he admitted to her.

"What do you mean you're not entirely sure?" She asked, confused. She looked through her notepads and found the one she had assigned to him.

"I can't even remember when was the last time I looked in a mirror. I know in barbershops they have a big mirror in front of you, but I requested to cover the mirror and that I would trust them. They did it for me, so I left him a nice tip," Liam answered.

"Is there a reason you do not look in the mirror?" She asked, intrigued while jotting down some notes. She noticed that he was watching her for a bit. She smiled and put the notepad down, and spoke again.

"If it ever makes you uncomfortable with me writing down any notes, don't hesitate to let me know. I will stop. I just do it to remember things and make a few observations to keep doing my best to help you every week," she told him. He managed a smile, something that was generally difficult for him.

"No, it's ok. I understand, and I am completely ok with it. But, honestly, I am surprised you haven't asked me tons and tons more questions about Faceless."

"Well, the man I am trying to help is Liam, not Faceless. Faceless retired. Although everything seems connected to Faceless, we will go at your own pace. Now let's jump back to the mirror," she said.

"Right. Well, I hate the face that I see. The face that I see disgusts me. The face that I see causes me to be angry," he confessed.

"It is the self-blame ideal," she stated as she wrote something else. Liam nodded while slightly moving on the couch.

"Alright, we can get back to the mirror later. How was your week?" Stefanie asked him. Liam scratched the tip of his nose and then clapped his hands once.

"Complete shit," he truthfully told her. She nodded at him, and rather than writing down anything, she elected to speak.

"What made it complete shit?" She asked. Liam let out a small laugh. For whatever reason, he was amused by her using the same language he had.

"I didn't know you cursed," Liam added.

"I am still a person like everyone else. I am not on any pedestal where I believe I am too good to curse. Plus, some people do not consider shit that bad of a curse word," she countered.

"Touche. Just for the record, I'm not judging. I can have a pretty big mouthful myself," Liam noted as he rubbed his mouth and took a big breath.

"For your week, why was it.. shit?" Stefanie reiterated.

"Well, where do I start? Almost every day, I had three hours or less of sleep. Constantly waking up with nightmares. I couldn't even do normal food shopping without feeling annoyed," Liam began. Stefanie leaned back on her chair with what Liam liked to think of as her thinking face.

"Do you know anything that may have prompted these nightmares?" Stefanie asked him.

"I've been having nightmares for years and years. It's mainly why I can't sleep."

"Are you comfortable with telling me what the nightmare was about?"

"It was something that actually happened. It was during a battle with the third-ever supervillain I faced," Liam answered.

"Tanner Brown," Stefanie softly added. Liam nodded and then leaned back on the couch.

"You did some research? Maybe you just remembered," Liam stated.

"I'll be honest; I did some research on Faceless. I wanted to update my knowledge, maybe understand things better."

"It's ok. I'm not judging you. On the contrary, I'm thankful for how you have treated me since I started coming here."

"That's why I do this job, to help people. I'm sure that's much like why you chose the superhero route once you acquired powers," she answered firmly.

"Yeah, except if I had to bet, I'd say you managed to help people," Liam deflected. Stefanie looked at him with her usual caring and gentle smile, which Liam was growing accustomed to seeing every time. It made him feel more welcomed, relaxed, and calmer. He was impressed by how little anything seemed to phase her. Perhaps with her job, she had heard it all by now.

"I'm sure you helped people as well. Even if you don't think you did. Here is a little moment of honesty from me. I'm never certain if I fully ever have helped someone or not. I don't always get to see the outcomes of these sessions," she clarified. Liam looked down at the ground, then shifted his gaze back to her.

"This nightmare, it was one of my battles with Tanner. I had been outside, trying to protect a house. He kind of pushes me so hard that I fly through the house. It all happened so quickly. When I returned to the house, people were very badly injured. They could still have lived at this point in time, but I... I decided to fly up, hoping Tanner would chase me in the sky and get him away from the house. Instead, I infuriate him and... he and..." Liam was lost for words. His eyes became teary. It was something Stefanie had not yet seen from him.

She hunched forward, paying close attention to his facial expressions and reactions. He attempted to speak again but was unable to compose any straight thoughts. Finally, he covered his face with his right hand and began crying. Stefanie remained quiet for a second, giving him some time. She then proceeded to lay back against her chair.

"We can talk about something else. Perhaps we can revisit your shopping experience," Stefanie suggested. Then, while still covering his face, he shook his head.

"You probably think I'm such a baby. Some big hero, crying his eyeballs out," he told her.

"There is nothing wrong with crying. It happens much more often than you realize, including the strongest people. Actually, I believe that the strongest of people are also the ones more likely to cry. It is a good way to relieve the pain, to let out some bottled-up emotions." Stefanie gave Liam a few more moments of quietness. She waited until he finally uncovered his face and began wiping away the tears with his sleeves. He sighed and then lay on the couch, his stomach facing up and his eyes directly looking at the ceiling.

"My mind was all over the place when I was shopping. I got pissed off just because there were so many different brands of the same exact pasta. All of them with different prices. All prices are relatively close to one another. What's the point of having so many choices, and yet the prices are just cents from one another?" Liam stated out of nowhere. Stefanie let out a giggle.

"Food shopping can be tough. Some people like specific brands for different reasons. Some claim they all taste the same, while others claim there are differences in tastes," Stefanie added.

"I think that the people that will say all of it tastes the same are just trying to fool themselves. I have definitely tasted differences in brands before. I am not trying to claim that one is good and the other isn't, but there are differences," Liam noted.

"Fair enough. Was there anything else of high note that maybe happened?"

"Not necessarily. Josh and Chaz haven't really been talking to me much. I think I upset them last week, but I guess there isn't anything I can do about that."

"What about the other two people you told me about, Henry and Tati?" Stefanie asked.

"They have been the same with me. I haven't noted any changes or oddities," Liam responded. He then moved again, sitting on the couch and looking at Stefanie.

"That's good, then. I feel like those are the two people whose opinions would matter more to you instead of everyone else in that workplace," Stefanie stated.

"You're probably right, as always," Liam admitted. His foot began to rapidly tap on the floor anxiously. He then jumped up and started pacing around the room. Stefanie didn't say a word. She simply observed him and began to jot down some notes. Finally, he returned to the same paintings he had been staring at the prior week as if admiring them for the first time again.

"Feeling any different about the pictures?" Stefanie asked. Liam didn't respond. In fact, he hadn't really heard her. He was lost in the picture with the silhouettes. He felt he'd been transported and was in some void, not a great one. Everyone was pointing and yelling at him. Stefanie tilted her head curiously, carefully paying attention to his reactions and emotions.

"Liam? Spot something different?" She spoke up. She still received no answer.

Liam was deep into the picture, still inside a void giving him shivers. He then heard a faint sound in the background. How could there be sound when the void was entirely empty? He heard it again, it still felt far, but it was getting closer. The sound of a woman calling his name, and then reality snapped back.

"Liam? Are you alright?" Stefanie asked. She was now standing right next to him. Liam turned his head to look at her. She looked worried, and he felt terrible about it. But nevertheless, he forced a fake smile before responding.

"Yes. I am sorry, I just got caught up daydreaming, thinking... Whatever you want to call it," he responded.

"It's alright. I just wanted to make sure that you were alright."

"Yeah. I am good. I do that from time to time. I think it's just a way for me to escape reality sometimes," He told her, then headed back towards the couch where he sat. Stefanie took one quick glance at the painting, thinking for a few seconds, and then returned to her seat.

"When I was a child, I thought I would be happily married and have at least one kid before I hit thirty. Now I am not far from thirty, and here I am fighting with my mind," Liam declared.

"Just because you are not married now and have no kids doesn't mean it still can't happen. Those things in life have no time frame," Stefanie pointed out. Liam laughed a little. Something she hadn't really seen either.

"Here is something sort of embarrassing for me to admit. I am terrified of having sex. I have no idea if I'd accidentally hurt someone terribly."

"Well, you've shown yourself you can hold a job without hurting anyone. But in the worst case scenario, if that option seems impossible, there are other ways to have kids with someone, medical ways, adoptions," Stefanie mentioned.

"That's true, but I'm not even concerned about that. It was just a thought that came to mind, I guess."

"What about your parents?" Stefanie asked.

"They've always been great parents, but I don't keep in touch with them that much. It's my own fault, though, not theirs. I kinda distanced myself from everyone I knew once I became Faceless. Huh, despite not liking the name, it seems to fit pretty well, huh?" Liam joked.

"It depends on how you want to look at it. Maybe Faceless doesn't have a face because he can be anyone who wants to help people. But Liam Lewis has a face, a personality, and a life," she told him. She was starting to grasp that he was human, just like everyone else. Years ago, he would be considered some extraordinary being that could get through anything. Still, underneath the plain mask, he was a human being. He wasn't much different than many other clients she's had.

"You're good, outstanding," Liam said, pointing at her.

"Oh? How so?" She asked curiously.

"You keep making me question things in my mind. Of course, I can't lie and say I am a changed man and everything is alright, but that certainly isn't your fault. It is my stubbornness for not fully listening," he told Stephanie.

"No one can fully change someone else. That person needs to want change, and even after that, it will take time. Questioning the negative in your mind is a step forward already, something that can continue to become more powerful as you practice it."

"When I searched for you online, I felt good about picking you. I was not wrong. Seriously, thank you. Even if it doesn't seem like it's doing anything to me, it is."

"That is good to know. Just keep at it. Reframe things in your mind, turn a negative into a positive."

"Are you going to set any goals up for next week? You know

shaving and a haircut could give someone a boost of confidence, so I would suggest trying and keeping the momentum going," Stefanie articulated.

"Hmm. I am not sure what sort of goal I could give myself."

"How about maybe, spending some time with people outside of work? It seems that your head just keeps spinning with thoughts when you are alone. Yet when you are not alone, even having to listen to everyone's pointless complaints, your mind seems to ease."

"Hmm. I don't know... I still feel iffy and scared about the whole idea," he admitted to her.

"That is the point, getting out of your comfort zone a bit. You can always make that your goal, and even if you don't make it for next week, that is ok. You can always carry the goal over until you finally do it. There is no shame in not doing it."

"Alright. I'll take a go at it. If Henry or Tati invite me out, I will say yes this time," Liam affirmed.

"Good! I'll look forward to hearing how it went even if it doesn't happen," Stefanie answered. It was then that Liam came to the realization that their session must have been coming to an end. She was already talking about goals for the following week.

"Next week, same day and time work," Liam quickly told her before she even had the chance to ask. Just saying it out loud made him feel sad. The week seemed to always drag on, and when the day finally came, it just went by so quickly. It was literally like blinking and missing an entire moment.

"We still have a few more minutes," Stefanie said with a smile.

"Oh, I thought I was done," Liam responded, relieved.

"Is there anything in mind you would like to talk about? These last few minutes could be a sort of free-to-speak whatever is in your mind time," Stefanie told him.

"Oh, wow... I wasn't expecting that. Well, how about if I played baseball, I would probably end up under investigation for steroids," Liam told her. Although Stefanie laughed, it was an interesting choice of topic.

"You think you would hit a home run every time up at the plate?"

"I mean, I'm not trying to speak highly of myself, but with my current strength, that ball would be going way, way out of the park," Liam told her.

"Well, yes. But there is more to baseball that you might be

missing. For example, you would have to make contact with the ball, which isn't always easy and simple when someone throws pitches over ninety miles per hour," Stefanie explained.

"You bring up a good point. I never really played baseball, so I'm only speaking gibberish," he answered.

"My dad used to watch a lot of baseball. So I spent much time with him watching plenty of games," Stefanie told him.

"That's nice. My dad didn't really care for sports, to be honest. He much preferred watching cooking shows. I know it probably sounds odd, but he loved learning new recipes and then cooking for my mother," Liam admitted to her.

"That's sweet. Are they still together?" Stefanie asked him.

"Yes, they have been happily together since the age of dinosaurs. It's really adorable when you see the two of them together, still as in love with one another as they probably were when they were young."

"Do you have any siblings?" Stefanie curiously asked him.

"No, I am an only child. When we were younger, my parents already struggled with me. They didn't want to have another kid and be unable to afford to take care of them."

"When was the last time you spoke with them?" Stefanie asked him. Liam leaned back on the couch and started thinking for a bit. "It's probably been a bit over two months, if I'm being honest. It definitely was before I started coming over here."

"Do they live far away?"

"No, not really. Just a state away. It's about an hour's drive," Liam then looked at the time and saw what he had been dreading. There were two more minutes in the session left. He stood up and forced a weak smile on his face.

"Thank you very much. This is doing me good. I still need to work through a lot, but I always look forward to Wednesdays now," Liam admitted to her.

"You're very welcome. I'm glad you are finding this to be helpful. I'll be seeing you next week then. Have a good night," Stefanie told him. Liam bowed his head and headed out of the door, closing it as he left the room. Stefanie picked up her notepad and started writing down a few notes. Maybe Liam didn't realize it yet, but she was beginning to see a difference in him week after week.

Chapter 8

Liam woke up Thursday morning feeling like the world had collapsed around him. That's how he had been feeling the last couple of Thursdays, knowing that he now had to wait another whole week to be able to go and see Stefanie. But, of course, if he'd mention that to anyone, they would start thinking he had a thing for Stefanie. Still, in reality, it was more about having someone he could be candid with and not feel as if he was being judged. He could talk about anything, even mentioning some of the dark things he had gone through when he was Faceless. Yet she did not treat him any differently.

'It's her job,' some people would probably tell him. Even so, there was something genuine about her. He'd read some reviews on other counselors that had him questioning, such as a lack of empathy, making them feel even worse about themselves. Yet, with Stefanie, he had not found a single negative review, which meant everyone else felt the same about her as he did. He was glad; she deserved it.

There had been one thing that was different this time, he had been able to get five hours of sleep, which was the most he had gotten on a single night since he could remember. However, he still had a few hours to go before leaving for work, so he approached his refrigerator and took out yogurt to eat.

He returned to the living room, where he sat on the couch, holding the yogurt in one hand and a spoon in the other. He looked to the side and saw that he still needed to move the journal from when he bought it. He shrugged his shoulders and then turned his gaze back to the yogurt. He finished eating it and then decided to do some push-ups and crunches. When he finished his short workout, he went into the bathroom and turned the shower water on to the hottest setting as he always did. He stood still, staring at the sink while waiting for the water to get hot in the shower.

The crack hadn't gotten any bigger. He did his best not to grab hold of the sink and kept leaving it alone. Deep down, he knew it would only be a matter of time before he'd let his guard down. He had even put money aside for a new sink for when the time would come. Finally, he began to feel the steam fill the bathroom, and that's when he knew it was time to jump into the shower.

He stood just under the shower head as the water came down the back of his head. His face was looking downwards, his eyes closed. He was in an entirely peaceful void for just a few seconds. Still, then it all quickly went away, and the face of Tanner Brown looking up at him with his big menacing smirk appeared. He had just come out of the house with Liam still floating in the air in complete shock.

"This is your fault, you know. You thought you would outwit me. Have me follow you out of here rather than face me like a man. This is your doing. Their deaths were entirely in your hand. Maybe they could still be alive if you had come out and faced me head-on," Tanner told him.

"I... I... I didn't do this... You had a choice!" Liam yelled back at Tanner. The faceless mask was covered in dust, which he wiped quickly just as Tanner began looking around.

"Since you want to stay up there, I guess I will move on to the next person," Tanner stated. Liam began to feel the veins pop out from his own neck. Anger began to consume him, and he quickly flew straight towards Tanner, punching him in the face so hard that Tanner flew against a poll.

Liam opened his eyes again, and he was back in his shower. He was breathing heavily, unable to concentrate, his mind being all over the place. Liam recognized that he was having an inner panic attack. He had to take a few slow deep breaths before feeling calmer. He turned the shower off and left the tub. Of the six supervillains he ever faced, only two were absolutely terrifying. Tanner was the second one of those. He got dressed while his mind raged with numerous thoughts. How will work be? Could he ever again have a normal life? What if a way to reverse his powers was found, and he chose to do it, could he simply forget everything else and move forward?

He had so many questions, and all of them were driving him insane as he had answers to none of them. So finally, he decided to leave the house early. He would burn time by driving around, perhaps even grabbing a coffee before heading to work. Once at work, nothing of note happened. The same would be said for the following few days.

By Tuesday, Liam felt he would fail with his goal. A couple of times through the week, he had worked a speech in his head to invite Henry and Tati to hang out with him. Still, he backed away from actually doing it every time he saw them. He could imagine Stefanie telling him, 'you're thinking about it too much.' It was true; he was. Finally, he was ready to go to work, and as he closed the door, he sighed.

He recalled Stefanie telling him that it was ok if he failed. There would be no shame. However, he did not like to fail himself. So, he got inside his car and turned the engine on. Then, he started driving away as his usual relaxing music started to play. The weather was a little warmer today, which made things a little more bearable. Yet, they were calling for one last snowstorm the following day, and they would start seeing the weather warm up week after week.

He parked his car in the same spot he usually parked. Like every other day, he was the first one there for his shift. Rather than going straight inside, he turned the music a little louder and leaned back against his seat. He started seeing several other colleagues pull into parking spots and walk inside. For once he wouldn't be the first one inside, and most likely not the first to clock in as well. That was something different, right? When there were only about five minutes until his starting time, he shut off the engine and exited the car. Josh and Mike were in the front of the building as usual, holding a cigarette, most likely talking about someone.

Although Liam didn't want to be near them, he knew he would have to walk right by them to get inside. So he decided to walk as slowly as possible, hoping they would head inside before he reached the door. But, unfortunately, it was not to be. The both of them were staring at him. It was as if they were waiting for him, they wanted him to cross paths with them. Inside his head, Liam was sighing and rolling his eyes. What could they possibly want with him? He then stopped, just as Josh walked up to him about to speak.

"You know Mason's bar down the street from here?" Josh asked him.

"Yeah, I've driven by it plenty of times," Liam quickly responded.

"They have karaoke night tonight. Come out with us unless you want to be an old man and go home and sleep," Josh told him. Liam sighed. He really didn't want to. Liam was about to decline the offer, but then he remembered that this could be an opportunity to accomplish his goal. Even if it wasn't the people he had hoped for, it was still better than nothing.

"Sure, I'll go," Liam reluctantly answered.

"Good. Karaoke starts at nine. We leave at eight-thirty, so we can go there straight from work," Josh told him.

"Alright, I'd rather go by my house first and shower before heading there."

"Whatever, we will be there," Josh responded. The tone of his voice insinuated that he was not expecting Liam to show up. Liam was alright with that. He would prove them wrong. Unlike them, though, he did not want to go out looking all sweaty and smelly from work.

The day felt like it was dragging. Liam wasn't sure if it was because he was looking forward to meeting with Stefanie again the following day or because he felt anxious about going out after work. Either way, he made it through. A few times, Josh insulted him throughout the day, saying things like, 'You're going to be a little girl and not come, are you?' Or 'Come see real girls. They are much better than going home and watching your porn.' Somehow he thought he was funny, though Liam was confident that no one ever found him funny. They all just pretended to laugh. Liam, though, never even made any attempt to laugh. He would just nod and focus on his job.

The time came, and Liam was one of the first ones to leave. Henry and Tati had both been off that day, so he didn't even have them to talk to and get their optimism for the day. Liam drove straight home from work, and the first thing he did was turn the shower on. Then, while letting the water run to get it hot, he ran over to his room to pick out the clothes he would be wearing. He placed them neatly on his bed and returned to the bathroom, undressing and jumping into the shower.

Once inside the shower, he did as he usually did. He stood under the shower head, allowing the water to hit his skin at full force. This time his visions were of things that could happen tonight. The first vision he saw was Josh and Mike being the most popular people in the bar as they both pointed at him and started laughing at him. The following image he saw was Josh pushing him to a breaking point. Liam lost control of himself and punched Josh so hard that he immediately fell to the ground dead.

Dark, he thought. Yet it was always something he feared. He then recalled what Stefanie had told him. Being at his job for a year, no accidents had ever happened. She was right. He did have some excellent self-control. Sometimes he wasn't sure that's what it was, but he needed to make himself believe it.

By the time he turned off the shower, he had spent fifteen minutes there. He laughed to himself. Josh and Mike must have been talking plenty of shit about him right now. Telling each other that they had been right; Liam wouldn't show up. Liam smirked. He was going to prove them very wrong soon. In fact, proving them wrong was currently driving his motivation to go even more. He walked over to the sink and combed his hair without looking at the mirror. He tried to feel it with his hands to see if it felt fine and then hoped for the best. He returned to his room, wrapped around his tower, and dressed.

It was a quarter to ten when he left his house and started the car engine. The sun was gone, and the moon was nowhere to be seen. The clouds had moved in. He didn't recall when it was supposed to snow, only that it was coming. It didn't matter to him either way. Having the following day off would be nice, and no matter what storm hit them, he wouldn't miss his appointment with Stefanie.

After driving for about ten minutes, he went past the bar. Unfortunately, the little parking lot beside it was already full. It was even difficult to find street parking. However, he did manage to get a spot after circling around for roughly five minutes. Finally, he turned off the engine and quickly left the car, not before making sure it was locked.

The letter's that read 'Mason's Bar' were fancy and lit up. Liam came to the realization he had never gone inside before. But, then again, why would he have? He didn't drink, something that immediately came to mind. *Bars have soda,* he thought as he approached the door. A bouncer was standing there. The man was big with a brutal look on him. Even his facial expression showed that he meant business like someone had already pissed him off enough for the day. Liam understood; it was supposed to be intimidating to anyone going in, but it didn't work for him. On the contrary, Liam knew how easily he could bring the man down. Still, the average person would certainly have trouble doing so.

"Do you have an ID?" The bouncer asked him with a deep and rough voice. Liam reached for his wallet and handed the man his driver's license. He would do his part and keep the peace, despite having no plans to order alcohol. The bouncer handed him back his driver's license and nodded at him while pointing to the door. Liam faked a smile at the man and opened the door. The moment he stepped inside, he could smell boos everywhere. The bar was quite full, which was extraordinary for a Tuesday night.

Were people really so bored on Tuesday that they had all decided to go to the bar? Was karaoke really such a big deal? Liam couldn't figure it out, so he continued looking around to locate Josh and Mike. He was confident that they would both be drunk by now. They had over an hour head start over him. Although he did want to see the look on their faces once they saw him. He looked towards the bartender and saw a tall black man, with a clean-shaven face and a smile that showed his perfect clean white teeth.

He then finally spotted Josh and Mike. They were near the microphone staring into a couple of women who looked to be half their age. Josh was the first to notice Liam and raised his glass before he walked toward him. As expected, he looked and sounded drunk, and so did Mike, who had closely followed Josh towards him.

"Hey! You came! Balls finally dropped, huh?" Josh laughed at himself. It was getting more and more difficult for Liam to hide the fact that he found none of it amusing it.

"This mother fucker right here is going to be singing next," Josh told Liam as he put his arm around Mike.

"What song are you singing, Mike?" Liam asked, without actually being curious at all.

"Your mom!" Mike answers much like a juvenile.

Maybe next, he will make a yo mama joke, Liam thought while Josh and Mike both laughed.

"Go get a drink! I'm going back to those girls right there," Josh told him before softly punching Liam on the shoulder. Josh walked away, and Mike followed him. Liam began feeling that neither of them would pay much attention to him. *All for the better,* he thought while turning towards the bar. He took a seat on an empty stool and began looking around. At one table were two people: a man and a woman. Their heads were very close to each other. Both appeared to be tipsy already, and in no time, they were exchanging saliva.

At another stool, another man had attempted to start talking to a couple of women minding their own business, but he was quickly turned away. Then, across from him was a man looking at the television. The man looked like some kind of predator, not much different from Josh or Mike, for that matter. Then the bartender came towards him.

"What can I get for you?" The bartender asked gently.

"I'm going to have a soda," Liam told him. At first, the bartender gave him a funny look, to which Liam forced an awkward smile.

"I know, I know. I'm at the bar, you can still charge me for an alcoholic drink, but I just don't drink. I only came because someone invited me," Liam explained.

"You came with friends, then?"

"I wouldn't really call them that," Liam admitted. The bartender let out a laugh.

"Thank goodness. I saw who was talking to you over there. No offense to you since I don't really know you, but I think they're both pricks," the bartender admitted to him.

"No offense taken. I feel the same way. My therapist suggested I try hanging out with someone outside of work."

"I'm sorry it ended up being those two. Lucky for them, my wife has kept me from kicking them out."

"Your wife?" Liam asked curiously.

"Yeah, my name is Cole Mason. My wife is Teresa Mason. We own this bar. She told me that if I kicked out everyone just because I didn't like how they talked about people, I wouldn't have any customers. So if they ever start touching or harassing my customers, I will drag them out personally."

"That would actually be quite entertaining. They're both losers, having some sort of mid-life crisis," Liam told him. The bartender smiled and handed Liam his soda.

"I'll charge you for the soda. I respect your reason."

"So you and your wife own this bar? That must be nice."

"Yeah, we both decided to invest in it. It's actually been expanded. It was really little when we started. She and I were the only two employees at first. We didn't even have a kitchen."

"That's great," Liam told him as he sipped his cup.

"Technically, I don't even need to work in the bar itself, but I enjoy being here. Plus, it keeps the work morale up for everyone else. I can cover if they need a day off or a vacation. We have come a long way. Our turnover rate is nearly nonexistent, either. Can't complain about life, you know."

"Every time I drive by, the parking lot is always full. People like coming here," Liam pointed out.

"Oh yeah, we have a lot of regulars. Excuse me a second," Cole told him as he turned to help another customer. Liam was thankful that the speakers for the karaoke weren't loud enough to block others from having conversations. Yet, it was still loud enough to hear others singing.

Mike was holding the microphone, and Josh was approaching Liam.
Fuck. Stay there, you shit face. Please stay away from me.

"Hey, what are you doing? Why are you not joining us over there? You see the boobs on those girls. Holy shit, what is wrong with you? Just sitting over there. Sheesh, man, you're fucking weird," Josh told him, feeling insulted. He turned around and returned to where he had previously been.

"Isn't he nice," Cole spoke, returning to the counter. He put both hands on the counter while slowly gazing around the bar, ensuring everything was going well.

"Even at work, he's a jackass," Liam said.

"I don't doubt it," Cole responded.

"Did it cost tons of money to open up the bar?" Liam curiously asked him. Cole thought for a few seconds before responding.

"It was a bit, but my wife and I put our money together and went for it. Of course, it was even extra because we went and got insurance."

"Insurance, huh," Liam softly mentioned.

"Yeah. I had a friend who owned a small convenience store. I told him repeatedly to get insurance, but he wanted to keep being cheap."

"What happened?" Liam asked. All of a sudden, he felt as if his guts were twisting. Somehow he had an idea of what might have happened.

"It got completely fucked up." Cole began telling him. Suddenly, Liam could feel the sharp pain going through his chest. He had a bad feeling about what he was about to hear next.

"How so?" He softly asked while sipping some of his soda.

"Well, Faceless was engaged in a fight with some lunatic. A car was thrown by Faceless toward this lunatic, who basically dodged the car. Unfortunately, it went right through the building. Luckily everyone had already been evacuated in the block, so nobody got hurt."

"That's harsh. I'm sure you and your friend must hate Faceless," Liam said. Cole smiled while grabbing a piece of cloth and wiping the counter.

"My friend? Yeah, he does. Me, on the other hand, not so much. I had warned him to get insurance. They had purposely created new insurance companies when Faceless came into existence."

"Yeah, but imagine if your bar got completely destroyed by something like that," Liam explained.

"Well, firstly, I am insured, so money-wise, it wouldn't cause me to go broke. On the off chance I was not insured, I still wouldn't be mad. If the consequence of saving so many people was destroying my bar, then so be it. My wife and I would find a way and get back on our feet. We always do," Cole responded with a lot of confidence. Liam took a deep breath and looked toward Josh and Mike, though his thoughts were elsewhere. Something he would be able to talk with Stefanie about the next day.

Chapter 9

The day had finally arrived. When Stefanie opened the door for Liam, his hair was covered in snow, and his jacket was drenched. He quickly took off his coat, and rather than placing it on top of the couch as usual, he put it on the back of another chair behind the sofa. He sat on the couch and watched as Stefanie also took a seat while getting hold of her usual notepad. She had her usual smile, something he had grown fond of seeing.

"Tell me about your week," she kicked things off.

"Nightmares of one of my battles with Tanner continue to return," he started.

"Is it the same battle as last time?"

"Yes, it is," he quickly responded. He was starting to feel a little thirsty. Unfortunately, he hadn't brought any water with him, something he decided to note for his next visit.

"Do you feel like there is anything in particular about that battle that keeps lingering in your mind?" Stefanie asked. How did she know? No, she didn't know what precisely that battle was leading to. It was just that she was deducing that there must have been something more.

"I don't... I don't really want to talk about it," he told her.

"Ok, that's fine. Anything else happen this week?" She asked while writing down some thoughts.

"I, umm, got invited out by Josh and Mike. The two people I was hoping I wouldn't," he told her.

"Did you decline them?" She casually asked while adjusting her glasses.

"I actually did not. I really wanted to, but that was last night, and I didn't want to fail my goal. I didn't get to see much of Henry and Tati this week. So when they asked yesterday, I decided to just say yes," he responded nervously.

"That's interesting. How did it go?" She asked, intrigued, while writing down a few more notes.

"They are both despicable people," Liam answered. She laughed and then nodded.

"Right, but you had already mentioned that even before. I mean, did an accident happen? Did anyone get hurt?" She asked, feeling confident that nothing terrible had happened.

"No, actually, it went very smoothly. I ordered a soda. I thought the bartender would make fun of me for it."

"Did the bartender make fun of you for it?"

"No, we actually ended up talking. He and his wife own the bar," Liam answered positively.

"Interesting. So not only did nothing bad happen, but you were also able to be engaged in a conversation with someone other than the people you had gone with," she reiterated to him. Liam knew what she was trying to do. She wanted to keep reinforcing the fact that nothing negative had really happened, that, in fact, something normal had actually occurred. He appreciated her attempt, but whether it would work or not would have to be seen.

"Yeah, he was a good guy. He told me a story, though," Liam admitted.

"What story did he tell you?" Stefanie asked.

"His friend lost his business because of a fight I had with one of the villains," Liam explained.

"He has a grudge against Faceless? If so, let us remember here that you are Liam Lewis and no longer Faceless. So despite if people feel right or wrong about Faceless, you are Liam."

"No, actually. He says he doesn't hold it against Faceless. I mean, his friend does, but not him. He said that even if it cost him his bar, he wouldn't be mad as long as it meant that more lives were saved," Liam answered. His eyes began gazing around the room again. Stefanie had figured out by now that when he did that, it was a reaction to his anxiety spiking. She knew that soon enough, he would probably stand up and walk toward the paintings. And right on point, he did just that.

"See, many people don't see Faceless the way that you do. Are there people out there who probably see him in a more negative light? Sure. Remember, though, there are probably people out there that see me in a negative light as well," Stefanie reminded him.

"Somehow, I doubt that. You seem empathetic and caring. Can't possibly imagine anyone thinking ill of you," Liam spoke as he approached the wall with the paintings. He immediately raised one of his eyebrows.

"Well, let's be honest, you only know me from these sessions," Stefanie pointed out.

"I've been meaning to ask the moment I walked in but haven't gotten around to it. So why did you change the paintings?" Liam asked. Stefanie smiled while putting her notepad to the side.

"I thought you hadn't noticed it."

"I did as soon as I walked in. The first thing I did was look at the wall."

"In truth, I have noticed how much you get drawn to the art, so I had been curious to see how quickly you would notice the change."

"Interesting," he added.

"What is interesting?" Stefanie asked, intrigued.

"These paintings seem to just be a bunch of colors thrown together. I can't really see any significance to them."

"We all can have different interpretations of paintings, same thing with life. Based on our sessions, for example, I can say that you do quite a bit of mind reading. You assume what people are thinking or may think of Faceless. Then you also do a lot of self-blaming. You make everything that happened while you were faceless to be your fault. It is all understandable, which is why we are here, to work on all that."

"Are those things even fixable?" Liam asked her while concentrating on the many different colors on the painting. It felt weird to him, but there was something about the image itself that soothed him.

"What is really fixable in life? Our minds are all very complex things. It will always be a work in progress. It'll never be simple or easy. One must always put work into it. Even if it doesn't get one hundred percent fixed, it does not mean you can't learn to cope with it. It will make it easier to have control of your thoughts. Reframing things in your own mind simply becomes a reflex," she explained to him. His gaze never changed. He felt comfortable and relaxed, but how could colors just do that?

"I'm sorry, I am listening... I just feel... " I don't know how to explain," he started talking.

"Relaxed, perhaps?"

"Yeah," Liam slowly responded. Stefanie leaned back on her chair while grabbing her notepad. She was going to give him the time he needed. She wondered what went on inside his head. She was even more curious to know how he used to be before acquiring his powers. How much being Faceless had changed the person Liam was before. She observed him a little longer as he appeared mesmerized by the painting.

"Tanner, he was awful. He would kill without hesitation just to get a reaction out of me. He'd tell me that the blood was on my hands, that it was my fault," Liam started talking slowly. Although it was hard for Stefanie to see, his eyes had become watery. Even as he spoke, there was a more significant weakness to his voice that hadn't been there before.

"He was only saying that to get to your head. Manipulation tactics, I should say. You never made those choices. It was Tanner that made those choices, and Tanner alone. He could have easily bypassed the choices he made and only confronted you. But, instead, he chose to murder those people, hoping it would bring you down and give him a chance to win," Stefanie explained.

"It's not that it did not bother me back then, but it seems to haunt my mind a lot more now. Maybe it's because I faced two more villains in seven months that year and didn't have time to think about it as much. Now all I have is time. Even when I went out last night, Faceless came up."

"Perhaps. But the objective isn't to forget Faceless existed. Unfortunately, that's impossible. The public won't let it die out," Stefanie added.

"Then what is the final goal?" Liam asked. He finally turned around to face Stefanie again.

"To forgive yourself, to forgive Faceless, to have balanced and forgiving thoughts about yourself," Stefanie told him. Liam walked towards the couch again and took a seat. Part of him wanted to tell her she was wrong, that it was impossible, that she didn't know. He did not deserve to forgive himself, and he didn't deserve anyone to forgive him. After a few moments, though, he decided against it. He didn't want to insult her. She was only trying to help. It was him that was not listening as much as he should.

"I don't know if there is forgiveness for Faceless and me," Liam said.

"Why do you feel strongly about that?" Stefanie wondered. Liam leaned back on the couch, sighed, and then closed his eyes briefly. The sofa was comfortable enough for some thinking. Finally, after a few seconds of silence, Liam began to speak.

"Tanner Brown. The battle I keep having nightmares about."

"What about that battle?" Stefanie asked.

"Well..."

* * *

Tanner stood back up after hitting the pole reasonably hard. His face was cut with blood dripping. The smirk on his face remained as he shook the dirt off his shirt. Tanner then dashed towards Faceless, swinging his fist high. The attack was blocked, and the two exchanged blows toward one another. They continued back and forth until Tanner found an opening and kicked Tanner in the stomach hard enough to send him flying through yet another building.

The moment Faceless started going through the brick walls, everything began to feel like one big nightmare. Suddenly he was no longer certain if he could win this battle. He even thought he had heard a faint scream for a second, but it was all too loud to tell for certain. His head saw stars just as he hit some wall and fell to the ground. His face felt bare. The mask had dropped a few inches ahead of him. He stood up, still feeling a little dazed. He shook the dust from his clothes and then grabbed his mask. As he put the mask on, he noticed a kid, no older than five, walk into the room. The kid looked to the side and began crying. He then looked at Faceless.

"You killed my momyyyy," the kid said. Faceless moved his hands forward and then looked to his left, where he saw a woman's body under a lot of debris. He froze in shock.

* * *

"When I got punched into that building, the impact was so large that the debris killed the woman. The kid was lucky that he hadn't been in that area at the time," Liam told Stefanie as he covered his face with both hands. The words, 'you killed my momyyyy' had been haunting him ever since. Now they were just replaying over and over inside his head. He shook his head. He tried to think of something else.

Rain, water, ocean, you killed my mommy... Fuck!

It had become unbearable, he quickly stood up, and Stefanie watched in surprise. She was seeing something she'd not seen from him, no doubt a panic attack from a traumatic experience.

"I got to go," he exclaimed. He rushed to the door, barely allowing Stefanie to stand and stop him.

"You still have time left in the session. We can finish; talk about it."

"I got to go," he said so fast that she barely managed to understand him. Then, finally, he opened the door and walked out.

"Don't do anything to hurt yourself. This will pass. " Call me if you need to," Stefanie shouted, worried. Liam did not respond. He simply shut the door and then froze for a couple of seconds. The same scene kept repeatedly playing in his mind, and no matter how hard he tried to think of other things, the same voice kept returning.

Henry, Tati, I killed your mommy... No, Tanner did; no, I did. It was my body that caused the debris. Damn it, what did I do? The door behind him opened slowly. He didn't notice, but Stefanie stood there watching him. Her face was filled with worry and horror at the same time.

"Fuck, I can't!" He exclaimed and then walked away. Stefanie stood there without a clue about what she could actually do.

* * *

Liam pulled to his street. He didn't know how he got there. He had spaced out his entire drive. He was breathing heavily. His emotions had not gotten any better on the drive. He exited the car as quickly as possible, slamming the door shut. Almost a little too hard. The walk to the door felt like an eternity. Once he made it to the door, he struggled a bit to unlock it with his key. His hand was shaking nonstop. Once inside the house, he ran to the bathroom, turned the shower on, and went to the sink.

You killed my mommyyyy, you killed my mommyyyy, you killed my mommyyy. It kept repeatedly playing in his head like a never-ending loop. Finally, he grabbed the sink tightly and slowly looked up at the mirror. His face was a complete mess. His cheeks were wet from the tears, and his eyes were red, as if he was having an allergic reaction. Even his skin was pretty pale. He then became angry at the sight. He was looking at a face that he could not stand to look at.

"You are a piece of shit," he said to his reflection. He then angrily punched the mirror. Pieces of glass shattered around the room, and now his reflection was distorted.

"AHHHH!" He screamed loudly, unable to get a hold of himself.

He slammed into the sink with his right fist, fully breaking it. His body began twitching as he turned towards the shower and saw all the steam coming out. He undressed rapidly and jumped in. Still twitching, he felt the hot water hit his skin. He moved the shower head and then sat at the end of the bathtub, wrapping his arms around his knees and his knees up against his chest. The water continued to shoot out of the shower head towards his face.

Time became irrelevant as Liam remained there twitching. The water had long ceased to be hot and had now become cold, but Liam had remained in the same position. He looked up when he heard his cell phone ring from inside his pants, lying on the floor. Liam reached out of the tub, grabbed the phone, and saw Stefanie calling him. He answered but didn't speak at first.

"Liam, I just wanted to check on you. If you'd like to talk, we can talk right now. After all, you never did finish your session," Stefanie gently spoke from the other end.

"I... am... not... good. Faceless, should have never existed."

"If Faceless didn't exist, the world could be under the control of super-powered lunatics. I understand that there were a lot of terrible things that happened. Just remember that a lot of terrible things also happen during war. Nothing is perfect. Everything is far more complex than we can ever figure out. Faceless is no more. It's just Liam now, and I've seen you go through changes. I've been feeling and seeing progress from you each week, and I know there will be more."

"I don't know if I'll be going anymore. It's not you; you are wonderful. I just can't be helped."

"Liam, you deserve the chance and the time to be helped. I promise I will do the best I can to make it happen. Do you want to come in an extra day this week? I think I have a few available time slots. I will put you down if you want to," Stefanie urged. She spoke with absolute worry, something he hadn't heard before.

"No, I'm going to go now," he answered apathetically.

"Liam, stay safe, alright? I'll put you down for next Wednesday at the same time. If you need anything or just talk, call me right away," Stefanie urged him. Liam moved the phone from his ear and looked at it. He ended the call without saying another word, threw the phone towards the floor, and returned to his catatonic state. His face looked up, allowing the water to hit him directly in front of his face. It had now become freezing.

Andre Pereira

Chapter 10

Stefanie was seated on her chair with one leg crossed over the other while her other foot was slowly tapping the floor with anxiety. In front of her sat another client of hers, Thelma. Thelma had big brown eyes, and her dark hair was tied into a bun. She had a stocky build, and her facial expression was angry.

"So, what's going on?" Stefanie gently asked.

"Fucking bullshit," Thelma responded rapidly. She leaned against the arm of the couch. Stefanie raised her eyebrows and put aside the notepad she had been holding.

"Oh, oh. Tell me about it," Stefanie said.

"Do you remember that bitch I told you about?" Thelma continued. Stefanie raised both eyebrows again, and with a gentle smile, she leaned forward. Her foot was still anxiously tapping. She hadn't felt it in a while, but there it was. She couldn't help but wonder if Liam was doing alright or not. She feared him possibly doing something reckless, and there was nothing that she could do to stop him.

"Eloise? The one that made up the rumor that you were sleeping around and made everyone call you a slut?" Stefanie finally answered.

"Yeah, that same bitch."

"What did she do this time?" Stefanie asked, leaning back towards her chair again. Stefanie hated to feel this way, but considering this was her last session of the day, she couldn't wait to get out of there. She wanted to check her phone and see if any news would pop up. She wanted to ensure her client was finding ways to keep himself in check.

"She told everyone my girlfriend had slept with this old dude from the fucking retail store."

"What does your girlfriend think about that?" Stefanie questioned.

"She asked me why I was so concerned about it if I knew it's entirely false."

"That could be a good point; she is doing this to get a reaction out of you. The important thing is if you know whether it is true or not. Many people probably don't believe her, either. They just play along to feel like they belong," Stefanie added.

"That's such bullshit," Thelma told her.

"It certainly isn't fair, and you have every right to feel how you

76

do," Stefanie told her. Unfortunately, the rest of the session felt like it had dragged on for Stefanie. She felt terrible for her client, who she knew was going through a lot herself, yet Stefanie's mind was made for the day. Nevertheless, she felt a sense of relief when their session ended.

Once she closed the door and was alone in the room, she quickly reached out for her phone and started looking for potential big news. There was nothing that came up. A good start. She didn't feel like heading home, so she texted one of her friends quickly to see if she could accompany her for a drink.

* * *

She met her friend, Jaymie, at the bar. Her friend was already holding a drink, seated by the stool watching the baseball game on the television. Stefanie took a seat right next to her.

"Sorry if I made you wait," Stefanie added. Jaymie smiled and gave her friend a hug.

"How have you been, Stef?" Jaymie asked with a smile as she alerted the bartender to add whatever Stefanie ordered to her tab.

"I've been alright, working a lot, you know," Stefanie answered.

"I bet you're doing an amazing job helping all those people! I take it that today was a fairly rough day?"

"You could say that," Stefanie answered and then ordered her drink.

"Do you want to talk about it?" Jaymie asked.

"You know I can't say much about my clients," Stefanie added.

"Well yeah, but you don't ever have to name names or anything."

"I'd rather just catch up and take my mind off work tonight. Thank you, though!" Stefanie told her. Jaymie had straight dark hair down her back. Her eyes were a beautiful shade of dark green, and as always, her eye makeup seemed on point.

"Of course. Other than work, anything else new with you?" Jaymie asked her.

"I have a boring answer. So that would be a no."

"Ah, no matter. I know how you are, Stef, always doing great things. I actually got promoted in my job last week. It hasn't become official yet, so I have told no one except for you."

"Oh wow, that's so exciting! Congratulations!" Stefanie told her friend while raising her glass. The two gently bumped each other's glasses together and then took a drink.

"Thank you, thank you. I've also put a down payment for a house, so I'm finally freeing myself from my parents' house. Finally, at last!" Jaymie jokingly said while raising her glass.

"That's amazing. You're doing a lot of great things," Stefanie mentioned.

"Well, amazing things for myself. On the other hand, you are doing many amazing things for other people," Jaymie told her. Stefanie laughed and then looked at the television where the baseball game was still going.

"How is your mother doing?" Jaymie asked as she also looked at the television.

"She seems to be doing about the same. She called me recently just to hear my voice. I do worry about her, though. It's not just that she's living alone, but she has no family living near her. I feel terrible about that, but she always insists on me staying here," Stefanie confessed.

"Typical mom. Perhaps it'll be easier for you to convince her to live closer to you than the other way around," Jaymie suggested.

"Maybe. She can be pretty stubborn sometimes," Stefanie replied.

"Like mother, like daughter." Jaymie and Stefanie looked at each other and then started laughing.

Stefanie enjoyed the remainder of the time she spent with Jaymie that night. It had been much needed. She gave her friend a big hug goodbye, and they each went back to their homes. Once inside her house, she grabbed her work cell phone and attempted to call Liam again. She received no answer. Instead, it went to voice mail. She walked out to her yard and looked in awe at the moonlight reflecting from the snow. Despite knowing that she was going to hate having to shovel the following day, at that current moment, she appreciated the calm and beautiful nature of the snow.

Chapter 11

A day had passed since his visit with Stefanie. The first thing he did in the morning was call his job and alert them that he wouldn't be there for a few days. He told them he wasn't feeling well. Part of him almost decided to simply quit, yet something had held him back from doing so. He didn't quite understand why, but something in him had told him not to do it. So instead, he stayed on his bed, holding the comforter up to his face. He wasn't sleeping, yet he wasn't awake either. It was like he was in between the two stages.

All of a sudden, Stefanie came to his mind. He felt terrible about how he had treated her and left things. It would perhaps be better if he simply stopped going to see her. She deserved far better and more respectful clients. This wasn't the first time he was going through something like this. He'd managed to overcome it before, then it would happen again sooner or later. He remained in bed, not paying attention to any activity on his phone.

The sun came and went, and Liam remained in the same bed. The only times he had left were when nature called. The following day was similar. He stayed in bed most of the day without much of an appetite. He attempted to block all the sounds around him as much as possible, but none mattered. His bathroom sink was still broken, so he would need to use the kitchen sink every time he needed to wash his hands. The shards of the broken glass still hadn't been cleaned. Anytime he had gone into the bathroom, he had stepped into the shards. His bulletproof skin had kept him from being cut. The bed was starting to feel like it was a part of him. There wasn't a greater comfort in the world at that point.

On the fourth day of his stay in bed, his mind began to see a little more clarity. He picked up his phone, only to learn the battery was dead. He connected it to the charger and headed over to the bathroom. He looked at the sink and sighed.

"I guess it's time to buy a new one," he told himself. He ignored the shattered mirror on the wall but grabbed a broom and dustpan to start clearing the glass on the floor. There was going to be some work ahead for him. Perhaps missing another couple of days of work would help him get caught up. Once he finished clearing it all up, he rechecked his phone. The battery had been charged to fifty-nine percent. It was good enough to check if he had missed anything.

The phone was powered on, and he patiently waited for the phone to be fully loaded. He had eleven missed calls from Stefanie. He took a deep breath, realizing it would be Wednesday again in just a few days. He would be missing that session. He didn't feel quite ready to talk to her or explain himself.

He then began looking through the search engine for new sinks and their prices. Money had already been set aside for it, and once he used it, he would start putting it aside again for the next sink. He was surprised the neighbors on the other floors hadn't said anything about him bringing so many new sinks in. Truthfully, he hadn't thought of an excuse to give if he was ever questioned on it. His car wasn't big enough for a sink, so he always had it delivered to his house. He wouldn't order it online, though. It was much better seeing it in person so that he would know exactly what he was getting.

Liam continued to scroll through different stores, trying to figure out which stores he would visit that day. *Why am I making this so much more difficult? Why can't I just go to where I always go, since I already know what they have?*

What fun would that be? For starters, you wouldn't waste as much time, and secondly, you may find something you have never found before. Maybe the cure for your unforgivable past!

Liam quickly set his phone aside, still attached to the charger. He covered his mouth with both of his hands and sighed. Frustration was starting to set in again, and at that point, he was tempted to lay down in bed again and put the comforter over himself. But instead, he tried to quickly change the thought process that he was going through.

I broke the sink again because I cannot control myself sometimes. Still, no one got hurt, and anger like that only seems to happen when I am alone because I am not concerned about anyone getting hurt. Therefore I care about people, so I wouldn't hurt anyone, not even accidentally. Maybe even now, I can get a more astonishing sink.

There was a soft and weak smile that came to his face. The idea of re-framing was doing the job a little. Perhaps not to perfection, as one would hope, but it did help deter him from entering another panic attack. He closed his eyes and took a few deep breaths while trying to think about the good things. Stefanie cared about him. It wasn't part of her job to call him eleven times to check up on him. Despite having some people he didn't quite like working with, others were good such as Tati and

Henry. Cole Mason was also a good guy; he had values and, most importantly, no grudges against Faceless.

As he reopened his eyes, he felt better than before. The progress was good. Although the techniques seemed obvious and straightforward initially, he had only really given any thought to them once he started practicing them, thanks to his therapy sessions. Just a few days prior, he had thought that he would never return, that everyone would be better off without his influence. At that exact moment, though, he was thinking of perhaps just missing a week to get his mind straightened out and then return to Stefanie. He jumped into the shower to get himself cleaned up. After getting dressed up, he headed out.

He drove to a new store he hadn't visited before to check out the bathroom sinks. He barely managed to find a parking spot and then headed inside the store. For whatever reason, it was reasonably busy. Luckily for him, most people were looking at washers and dryers instead of bathroom sinks.

Well, not everyone breaks bathroom sinks at the rate that you do, Liam.

Man, why are you so fixated on bathroom sinks? Why not go where you usually buy them and order the same one. What difference does it make?

Shut up.

In the same aisle, a couple was looking for 'the perfect sink,' in their own words. They looked young and had probably just bought their first house. Good for them; looking so excited over buying a brand new sink. Meanwhile, this was like a routine for Liam himself. He began to wonder how it would feel like to shop for something with someone you loved like that. Whether it was for a new house or a movie to watch that night. Such things did not seem like they would ever happen to him. But, regardless of how well he thought he had control of himself, there was no saying what could happen while sleeping.

He watched the couple for a little while. In a non-creepy way, as he would like to think. They were young and very much in love with one another. They couldn't keep their eyes off each other. The shorter woman was holding on to the arm of either her girlfriend or wife. He didn't know or think it was important to know. He still found it beautiful for two people to be so close to one another. Looking for a new bathroom sink was a nice, exciting bonding moment for them. He managed to get a genuine smile before focusing on finding a bathroom sink for himself. Perhaps his visits with Stefanie were starting to pay off. Somehow his mind always kept returning to Stefanie and what she would say to him.

He was challenging his thoughts more and was beginning to see an entirely different light on things. Seeing two people so happy together had helped him feel a little better inside. If he couldn't get a taste of it with someone else, then at least others got to. Maybe that was one of the solutions, putting himself out there to see other people living their lives in ways he couldn't. Give him hope for the world and maybe a little hope for himself.

He managed to find a sink that caught his interest for no particular reason. It was a little more than the previous sinks he had bought, but something about it called for him to buy it. Not a single thing extraordinary about it either. He just liked it and couldn't explain it. He placed his order on the sink and filled out the paperwork. They told him the delivery would be in two days, something he didn't mind. How could two more days without the sink hurt anyways? He then returned home, or as he liked to refer to it, the nothing-exciting land.

Each day kept passing. The sink was delivered on time, and like all the previous times, Liam put it together himself. Once he was done with the sink, he stayed occupied by doing push-ups and sit-ups and listening to more relaxing music. His mind started getting back together. He was on the right track. When Wednesday came, he skipped his appointment with Stefanie. He hadn't called her back yet to reaffirm anything. Part of him felt terrible. The other part didn't have it in him to talk to her yet. He needed to be sure he could handle this. Then it was Thursday, the day he was to return to work.

Work was certainly not where his mind would ever go into the most healthy state. He was reminded of it when he started working and had to hear Josh whining and complaining about Mike. Even Mike wasn't safe from Josh's trash talk, why would Liam feel that he was an exception?

"That fucking guy. Never works. Just spends the entire shift scratching his balls, then I have to catch up on his work. I'll tell you, nobody in this place works their ass more than I do," Josh told him with an aggravated tone. It was a pretty big lie. Josh himself didn't do much different than anyone else. Yet, somehow he felt that he was the greatest thing that had ever happened to that company. All Liam could do, was simply nod and let Josh talk it away. It was better that way.

"What about you, sick for a week?" Josh asked him.

"Yeah. I had never felt like that before. Didn't want to risk anyone else catching anything."

"Are you better now? Everything good?" Josh asked him, appearing to show some sympathy for once.

"Oh yes, I'm all good now," Liam quickly responded. He turned to see Henry and Tati walking together. They must have been going on their short break. He thought about some things briefly and then turned to face Josh.

"Hey, I'm sorry. There's something I need to do. I'll talk to you later," he told him.

"Ok, you go. I'm going to go and do the work for Mike as always," Josh complained. Liam nodded and gave him a fake smile. He then jogged to catch up with Henry and Tati.

"Hey, Liam! You're back. How are you feeling?" Henry asked him loudly and full of energy.

"Much better, thank you. Hey, I was wondering, would you two be interested in hanging out? Maybe a game night or going to a bar or something?" Liam asked them.

"Absolutely! Tati is coming over to my house tonight. My boyfriend is going to be there too. We will be having a game night or a movie night. You are more than welcome to join us," Henry told him.

"Yeah, I'll do that," Liam replied with a sincere smile.

"Perfect, I'll text you my address. You can come over straight out of work or whenever. We will probably be up fairly late anyways," Henry added.

"I'll probably go home, shower, and then head over," Liam said.

"No problem, we will see you tonight then," Henry told him. Liam noticed the friendly smile on Tati's face.

"Glad you're joining us," she told him.

"Me too," Liam admitted. He allowed them to head over to their break while he returned to work. At least Chaz was off that day, so he wouldn't have to listen to him deflecting the blame to everyone else. Liam then cleared his mind and focused the remainder of his shift on his job. His manager called him into the office a few minutes before he was finished.

Liam nervously sat inside the office while his manager looked through some paperwork on the desk. The manager then closed the binder and placed it aside. Finally, the manager raised his head to look at Liam.

"How are you doing? Are you alright?" His manager finally asked. Liam nodded slowly.

"Yes, I am doing much better than I was last week. Sorry that I missed an entire week of work. I know I'm probably in trouble," Liam nervously answered. The manager squinted, looking at Liam, surprised.

"You're not in trouble. I only called you to the office to make sure you are alright. I was worried, you have never missed work before. You're also one of the best workers here, so I just wanted to ensure that there wasn't something going bad over here," the manager told him. Liam exhaled in relief and then nodded a few times.

"No, no, it's nothing to do with work. I was just feeling terrible last week," Liam answered.

"I'm sorry about that. You know how Josh has a big mouth. He told everyone you had gone out with them after work and never returned." Liam almost wanted to laugh. But, of course, Josh had opened his mouth. Why wouldn't he? He always needed to be the center of attention.

"Oh no, I don't really respect him, but he alone wouldn't change much about work for me," Liam admitted.

"Alright, that's good to know. Hope you continue to feel better, and glad to have you back. I'm sure you're ready to go home. Your work is done anyways, so you can leave a little early," his manager told him.

Liam quickly stood up and shook hands with his manager while thanking him. Liam punched out when he was out of the office and drove home to shower. His car was making some weird noises, which he ignored for now. After parking his car, he ran into his house while trying to not use his super speed.

Once inside, the first thing he did was turn the shower setting to the hottest possible setting. It was like a ritual to him. He couldn't do anything less than the hottest possible setting. Next, he undressed inside his room and checked his phone. There was a text from Henry giving him the address to his house. Liam managed to smile and then returned to the bathroom, where he jumped into the shower. Usually, he would stand there for a long while, taking in the feel of the hot water. This time though, he tried to be as quick as possible. He had places to go and was excited about it, unlike when it had been with Josh and Mike.

It didn't take him more than thirty minutes to get completely ready to head out. Once fully dressed, he checked his pockets for his keys, phone, and wallet. He was content enough to exit the house after feeling all three items. He approached his car, using the controller to unlock the doors and jumping into the driver's seat. He put his key in the ignition and attempted to start the vehicle. He held the key for a few seconds, but all he could hear was the engine trying to turn itself on with no results. He laid back in his seat, frustrated. Of course, this would be happening now. It was the story of his life. Every time he started getting excited over something, it would immediately bring him back to reality.

Screw this, no!

This time he would not allow it to defeat him. He would not allow it to bring him down. This time it would be different. Sure, it was already nighttime, but it wasn't even nine yet. He could walk. Based on the address given, Henry didn't live far from him. All it would take was a twenty-minute walk. Sure, he hated the cold, and there was still lingering snow from the previous week, but he couldn't allow any of that to stop him. This time he would look at life and say, 'Fuck you. You can't stop me.' He would have to deal with his car issue the following day before work. If it wasn't solved, he could just walk to work despite it being about an hour.

It was cold, but not unbearably cold. The streets still had leftover snow from the previous week. As he continued to walk through the sidewalk, he took out his cell phone. He texted a message to Stefanie, 'Sorry for not reaching out sooner, sorry for skipping yesterday. If possible, could I please have an appointment for next Wednesday at the usual time? Promise to be there. Thank you.' He then turned off his cell phone and continued his walk in the middle of the night.

By the time he reached Henry's house, he had been walking for twenty-four minutes. Henry lived in an actual house rather than an apartment. The lawn and the roof were covered by snow, but the house was freed of snow, allowing its beige color to be admired. The house looked to be two floors from the outside. Liam walked up the four steps in front and gently knocked on the door. A few seconds after his knock, the door swung open with Henry standing on the other side.

"Liam! You came. That is so awesome!" Henry shouted out in joy. He appeared to be intoxicated already. He was wearing green shorts and mixed socks with a white tank top. Henry moved his hands, motioning for Liam to walk inside.

"Come on in, come on in," Henry rapidly said.

"Sorry, I'm a bit late. My car wouldn't start, so I walked here," Liam apologized.

"Ah! I would have... I'm a little drunk. My partner would have picked you up!" Henry stated.

"It's alright. It was a nice walk," Liam responded as he took several steps inside the house. He noticed a few pairs of shoes on the floor, and before even being asked to, he took his shoes off out of respect.

"Ah, you didn't have to do that," Henry clarified.

"It's quite alright. I don't want to be disrespectful," Liam answered. His voice was slightly lower than usual like an introvert would speak in larger gatherings. He followed Henry to the living room, where three other people were waiting for them. One of them he recognized as Tati.

"Liam, that tall skinny man right over there is my partner, Peter. Peter, this is Liam. You've heard about him," Henry started saying, then he looked towards Liam.

"I have talked so much shit about you... I'm just kidding. " You're one of the few people I can stand at work," Henry told him.

"That last part is true. He hasn't actually said anything bad about you,"

Peter concurred. He approached Liam and gave him a handshake. Henry then turned to the other person in the room. This woman must have been about five feet and two inches short, with a few extra pounds on her. Her nails were painted black, and her hair was dyed green and in a ponytail.

"That is Tati's friend Harley," Henry told him, slurring the words slightly.

"It's Charley!" Tati yelled out, followed by laughter.

"My gosh, Henry, you are so drunk," Peter pointed out. Henry started laughing and then threw himself onto the couch. Tati came rushing towards Liam, awkwardly standing and watching everything happening.

"How are you doing?" She asked him while taking a couple of sips from her cup.

"I am doing well, thank you. How about yourself?"

"Fantastic! Would you like a drink? I can grab you something," she mentioned.

"Oh, just a water or a soda," Liam answered quickly.

"Not a drinker, huh? I respect that. I think Henry has some sodas in his fridge. I'll go check for you," she answered before disappearing into the kitchen. He watched as Peter took a seat next to Henry. Charley smiled at Liam while lifting her glass up. Liam answered with an awkward smile and stepped into the middle of the room alongside everyone. Although it looked like they had been playing a board game, it did not seem like they would be finishing it.

Tati returned with a can of soda and handed it to Liam. He thanked her while grabbing the can. He opened it and drank a little bit from it. It tasted a bit flat, but he chose not to say anything. Instead, he raised the can and nodded as if he had just given a toast. Charley sat on the floor beside the table they had been playing the game on. Tati joined her shortly after. Tati pointed Liam to an empty armchair across from her and Charley. Liam nodded and took a seat on it.

"Thank you," she nervously answered. This was perhaps the most awkward and out of his comfort zone that Liam had felt in a while, despite trying very hard to hide his shaking and feeling like his heart would explode at any moment. Nevertheless, he still much preferred this to Josh and Mike's company.

"Liam, Liam, Liam, you doing better this week?" Henry drunkenly asked. Liam nodded alongside his answer, 'Yeah, it was just a rough week last week.'

"It happens. It happens to the best of us!!" Henry added.

"We missed you there. Josh started coming to us with his complaining and bitching. Can you believe it?" Tati joked.

"Oh my gosh, he is so annoying. I have no idea how you put up with him," Henry added.

"Henry and I were talking. We thought that you going out with them was probably why you missed work, you know, because of big pieces of shit they are," Tati added.

"I guess it wouldn't exactly be out of the realm of reality," Liam responded. They spent most of the night talking about work and other random things. Liam discovered that Charley and Tati had known each other since high school. No one else had ever wanted to be friends with them. Charley was a hairstylist. She actually enjoyed her job too. Tati was planning to return to school. She wanted to be a mental health counselor, something that intrigued Liam. Time passed by quickly, and with it, Henry passed out on the couch. It was close to two in the morning when Liam decided to leave and walk back home.

Tati had offered to give him a ride, but he had declined. He didn't mind the night. She was more concerned about him getting attacked, which he tried to downplay by telling her it was a safe walk any time of the day. After some resistance, she finally allowed him to leave on his own.

Once outside, he noticed that the moon and stars were nowhere visible. It was a bummer. He really liked being able to look at them. It somehow gave him a sense of hope. He started walking steadily, taking one step at a time. The streets were so quiet at night not even cars could be heard at that moment. He looked up at the street lights. One was a little dimmer than the others. He figured this is how many horror movies would probably start. He couldn't be sure since he hadn't watched movies in quite a long time.

He decided to take a different route home. He took a right turn and continued walking in the street filled with trash everywhere. He even heard a large gathering of rats by one of the dumpsters that he walked past. The smell was almost unbearable as well. He started to regret taking this route, he had simply wanted to explore new places, but this hadn't quite been what he had in mind.

He looked at the GPS he was using on his phone and noted the street name he was in. Then, he started hearing some rumblings, possibly an alley, coming from ahead. He took each step carefully. He then went to the alley where he had heard the rumblings and saw what was happening. Three dirty-looking men were pinning another man against the wall. One of them had his shoulder pressed against the victim's head.

None of them had noticed Liam yet. Liam's heart began beating at a rapid speed. He felt his muscles tensing up. He could feel the adrenaline rushing through him. He could stop them and not even break a sweat. It was then that he saw something flashing in his mind. He watched as the fist punched another man in the face, followed by voices in his head, *'He's going to have permanent brain damage. It's a shock that he isn't dead.'* Liam shook his head quickly and then turned around and began walking away. He grabbed his phone and dialed nine one one.

"Nine one one, how may I help you?" A voice spoke from the other end.

"Hi, I was walking home right now, and I just passed by a group of three men attacking another one in an alley. I feel as if the other man is in danger. I want to help, but I'm afraid they might attack me and be armed. The street name is Wolfing Street," Liam quickly said, then hung up the phone. He hoped that it would work and that they wouldn't trace his number and come looking for him either. He continued going home, trying not to think about what he had just witnessed, attempting to ignore that he was a true coward and how he could have helped the man but had chosen not to. He was an actual piece of shit.

Chapter 12

Liam quickly opened the door to his house and closed it just as fast. His heart was still racing and pounding. He hadn't even waited to see if the police had come to help. Instead, he kept walking without ever turning back. As he stood inside his house, barely able to breathe with his lungs tightened, he hoped everything had been resolved. He was hoping that everyone was alright. He had acted like a coward, frozen when someone desperately needed help. He quickly ran into the restroom and did his usual routine. He turned the shower to the hottest setting when he became too stressed and anxious. He glanced at his new sink, still in a brand-new shape. Unfortunately, the same couldn't be said about the mirror he had not replaced. He touched his chest while breathing heavily, trying to hold back his nauseous urge.

Once he saw the steam coming out of the tub, he undressed rapidly and stepped inside. He quickly started rubbing his face as the water hit him. He, indeed, had no worth in the world. How could he re-frame this situation? It was inexcusable. The man was being attacked by three other guys. The man had been helpless. On the other hand, Liam could have taken on all three thugs with a single arm and not even gotten scratched.

STOP!

He was thinking far too much about it. It was likely that the police had gone to investigate, and no one had gotten hurt. What if they had never arrived? What if the police had thought the call was a prank because he hung up so quickly? What if they were tracking the number and coming to arrest him instead? There were far too many what-ifs in his own mind.

Could he even return to Stefanie after all of this? What would she think of him? Even Stefanie wouldn't be able to spin this around in any sort of positive manner. Maybe therapy had been a mistake from the very beginning. It was making him think about his thinking a lot more. The best thing to do would be to quit now? No, he couldn't, though, could he? What if quitting would actually make things even worse? It was already a miracle that he hadn't lost self-control easily in the last two years while barely having any sleep. He would go, he decided. No, he wouldn't... Yes, he would. His next session would be in almost a week. It would be then that he would make up his mind on whether he would stay or not.

The last time he had practically walked out halfway through his session and then missed this week's.

He remained in the shower until the water became completely cold. It was then that he felt his adrenaline die out. After leaving the shower, he went into the kitchen and opened one of the cabinets. He carefully looked around and then grabbed a box of tea. He warmed up some water and mixed it with a tea bag. He took a sip of the drink when it was finished. He had never been a big fan of tea but was always told it could help with stress. Hopefully, it was true.

He walked over to his couch and almost sat on top of the journal that he still hadn't touched since throwing it there. For weeks he had neglected to write on it or even move it away. Rather than moving it at that moment, he moved and sat beside it. He stared at the blank television screen before him while sipping his tea.

That guy is dead because of you.

Shut up! He's not dead, the police came, they helped him. But, unfortunately, talking to himself inside his head was becoming too frequent lately, even more so than before. He wondered how bad of a sign that could possibly be.

He leaned back, tilted his head upwards, and took a couple of deep breaths. He began to note the imperfections of the ceiling. It was such a boring hobby without any real purpose, yet it still distracted him for a little bit. He quickly stood back up while grunting made-up words and returned to the kitchen. Liam put his mug on the table and went to his room. He dove into his bed and placed his head between two pillows. He already knew that there was no reality in which he would get any sleep that night.

Liam remained on his bed, almost as if he was paralyzed, for the remainder of the night. That was up until his cell phone's alarm went off. It meant it was nine-thirty morning, and it was time to start preparing for work. He slowly got out of his bed, feeling parched. He took small steps toward the kitchen as if he were someone without purpose.

He looked at the mug of tea he had left on the table. It was most likely cold by now. He hadn't even drunk half of it. He grabbed an empty glass and filled it with water. He drank it like he was taking a shot. After using the restroom, he returned to his room and looked for his laptop. He sat on his bed, opened the laptop, and began searching the web.

The first thing he typed was, 'Three men jump another man,' and he got a lot of unexpected results which had nothing to do with the previous night. Most of them were simply pornographic results. He then typed something else in the search bar, 'Wolfing Street news,' and clicked search. At first, it didn't seem like he would have much luck, but once he clicked the news tab, he saw an article from just three hours prior. He clicked on it.

'MAN IN SERIOUS CONDITION' was the title of the article. Liam felt his insides twisting and turning, causing him intense inner pain. He started to slowly read the article, 'Thursday night at approximately 2 A.M. The police received an anonymous call about a man being attacked by three other men. Police responded to the call only to find that the three assailants had fled the scene. One man was found near death after having been stabbed. The man was taken to the hospital but is still in serious critical condition. We will continue to update this article as we receive updates on the man's condition and the suspects.'

Liam quickly closed his laptop. Guilt ran through his spine while his insides punished him further by tightening up. Sweat began to pour down his face while his heart rapidly beat. Despite the man still being alive, he could die at any point. The worst of it was that he could have stopped it. He could have made a difference. In the past, he would have done something. He would have made a difference. Now, he was nothing but a weak coward. Unworthy of any powers he had ever received.

Liam, you are a piece of shit.

I know. I am.

If that man dies... it's your fault.

I know. I know.

You are a poor excuse for a superhero. Oh, wait, sorry, former superhero.

I know. I know. Now shut the fuck up.

"FUCK!" Liam screamed out loud uncontrollably. He moved his hands to his face, tentatively watching them as they trembled uncontrollably. Tears started to come down his eyes, and he quickly fell to his knees. He began to hyperventilate. He attempted to calm himself down by closing his eyes and trying to focus on something more positive. Nothing seemed to come to his mind at first, and then Stefanie came to mind, followed by his life before obtaining his powers. Things had been so much simpler then.

He heard his phone make a sound and slowly turned his head and opened his eyes simultaneously. He got up feeling slightly calmer despite his heart racing and his body trembling. He approached his phone and saw that he had received a reply from Stefanie.

'No worries. Just hope everything is alright. I have you down for Wednesday at the usual time. Looking forward to seeing you back.' He stared at the message for a little while before putting the phone away. He would just have to try and figure things out until Wednesday and then force himself not to skip another session. Perhaps all of this was punishment for missing an entire week. He had allowed weakness to control him.

His first instinct was to call out of work and spend the remainder of his day at home, but then he reminded himself that he had already missed a week and had only been back at work for one day. So he forced himself to prepare and then recalled that his car hadn't started the previous night. So he went outside to start it again but had no better luck.

"Piece of shit," he said softly while taking out his cell phone. It was time to request a ride. He wasn't a fan of the idea, but after the previous night, he wasn't in the mood to walk either. After waiting about twenty minutes at his steps, the ride finally arrived.

Liam chose to sit in the back instead of being in the passenger's seat and remained quiet the entire ride. Upon arriving at work, he thanked the driver and made sure to tip him well on the app. He attempted to stay away from everyone as much as possible. At one point, Tati checked on him to ensure everything had gone alright the previous night. He, of course, lied to her but also agreed to let her give him a ride home after work that day.

At one point in the day, he received a call from the police department with a few questions. His nerves returned to him as he stepped outside to take the call. He found a spot a few feet away from the building to take the call, where he cooperated as best as possible.

"The night you called us, and then you simply hung up," the officer said.

"Yes... Yes... I was nervous. I thought one of them might see me on the phone and then try to attack me. So I wanted to get out of there as quick as possible," Liam lied.

"Why were you out so late at night?" The officer asked him with a little attitude.

"I had gone to a friend's house. I stayed there a bit late and then

93

decided to walk back home. But, unfortunately, my car is currently not working."

"One of your friends couldn't give you a ride?" The officer asked him, sounding doubtful.

"Yes, one of them volunteered. I did not wish to be any trouble to them. I also happen to like walking, so I declined the offer. My biggest mistake was taking a different route home than usual," Liam admitted.

"Most people would not want to walk at that time of the night, regardless of which route they took," the officer challenged him. Liam moved the phone away from his face and then slowly inhaled some air. He was becoming frustrated. Somehow he did not think the officer was going to let this go. Now that he thought about it, he'd made himself seem sketchy. Had he made the wrong move by calling the police? Had he not, the man himself could have ended up dead.

"I understand, officer, but not everyone is the same," Liam responded rudely. He could sense that the officer did not find it amusing.

"Perhaps you would like to come to the station and talk about it," the officer told him with authority.

"I don't see why I would. I have committed no crimes, broken no laws. But, I saw something bad happening, I did my duty as a civilian and called the appropriate authorities. I have co-operated in this phone call with your questions," Liam quickly responded. He didn't believe a good portion of what he had just said, but he felt as if it was what he needed to say. Liam needed to stay strong and stand his ground. The last thing he wanted was to start being put in police stations and interrogated. Yet, he quickly began to question his own instinct. Perhaps he was making the situation worse for himself.

"Keep your phone on and answer the calls," the officer told him before hanging up. Liam could tell the man was annoyed; somehow, he felt this was not the last time he would hear from Officer Dante. Not much else happened for the remainder of the day. He allowed Tati to give him a ride back home. Once home, he first grabbed his laptop and checked for the same article from earlier. There had been no further updates, the police still had no suspects, and the victim was still in critical condition. He closed the laptop, frustrated, and laid back on the bed.

With each day that passed, his routine became similar. The first thing he would do in the morning was check for any updates. Then he would check again before leaving for work and once more at night. The next time he was off from work, he found an open garage to which he towed his car. Fortunately for him, the issue hadn't been too problematic and was fixed in just a few hours. He would anxiously check his cell phone daily, expecting another phone call from Officer Dante. He started to fear maybe even getting a visit from him at his job or home. To his relief, it didn't seem to be as each day passed.

It was on a Monday night that the article was finally updated. The man was no longer in critical condition and would live, much to Liam's relief. He fell back on his bed, able to breathe a little better. Maybe now he wouldn't have to worry about the police coming after him as much. Perhaps they would just wait for the man to rest and then ask him the needed questions.

This was good news for him, despite still being disgusted with himself. The day to go see Stefanie was quickly approaching. The last time he had seen her was two weeks prior, she was probably going to have a lot of questions for him, and he needed to prepare mentally. He found himself in a better state of mind that night as he waited to fall asleep.

Despite listening to more of Josh complaining and then Chaz complaining on Tuesday, he managed to get through the day. Back at home, he did nothing besides sit on the couch holding a mug of hot chocolate. He anxiously awaited his appointment the following day as the hot chocolate became colder and colder.

Chapter 13

Only two weeks had passed, yet it felt like an eternity since Liam had last seen Stefanie. She let him inside the room, and the first thing he did was look at the paintings on the walls. They were back to the original paintings from the first three weeks. He then looked back to Stefanie.

"You changed them back," Liam noted. She gently smiled while walking over to her seat to grab her notepad. It was a smile that Liam had missed for sure.

"Well, when I changed them, it seemed to bring negative results. Thought maybe I should change them back," she admitted. As usual, she sat down and crossed her legs, and then Liam realized she looked different. Generally, she would adjust her glasses, but she wasn't wearing them this time. How could he not have realized the moment he saw her? Perhaps it was because she was beautiful with and without them.

"Your glasses are gone, too," he quickly stated while sitting on the couch.

"Wearing contacts today," she answered cheerfully.

"Cool. You can pull off the glasses, and no glasses look," he told her with a gentle smile.

"Well, thank you. It's been a couple of weeks since you were last here. What's been going on?" She asked him directly. He forced another smile before gazing around the room, seeking any more potential differences.

"Well, first, I'd like to say it wasn't the paintings. It was just me. I seem to go through waves of inner attacks like those."

"There is nothing wrong with that. It happens. What happened after that?" She calmly asked him with the same calm demeanor that she always had.

"Well, I took a week off of work. The first half of the week was me lying around in self-pity. Then I started to get myself back together and out there. I had broken my sink at some point, and well...my mirror broke as well because I looked at it...."

"You looked at your mirror, and it broke? Those are some kind of powers," Stefanie interrupted. Liam couldn't help but laugh.

"No, no. I punched the mirror," Liam explained.

"Punched the mirror? Were you just angry at that particular time?"

"Looking in the mirror made me angrier," he admitted.

"How come?"

"Because I saw my face."

"Your face angers you?" She curiously asked while writing down something.

"Well, I felt disgust towards myself, anger for everything that's happened. I think I may have somewhat mentioned this before," Liam responded. Stephanie nodded with a 'Huh, huh,' tone.

"We have, but it's good to see you being able to talk a little more about it. So that was about your first week, and then what?" Stefanie continued.

"Well, I did finally ask Henry and Tati to hang out. So I ended up hanging out with them at Henry's house. Except my car stopped working right when I was going to head there, so I walked."

"That's great. How did that go?"

"It was a bit weird, I admit, not on Henry or Tati. They were good hosts, good people. I just... I felt like an intruder."

"Why did you feel that way?"

"They all knew each other. They had already planned on hanging out that night before I had gone to invite them. Maybe they didn't want me there."

"If they didn't want you there, why would they have invited you to go over?" Stefanie challenged him. Liam smirked a little and nodded a tiny bit.

"Because I had asked them if they wanted to hang out," he finally responded.

"If that was the case, wouldn't they simply tell you that they were busy that night and to do it another night?" Stefanie remarked.

"Well... umm... I guess... yeah..." Liam was unable to compose a complete response.

"You had to walk to their house. Did you fly back home that late at night, then?" Stefanie asked. Liam shook his head.

"I want to avoid using my powers no matter what. So I decided to walk even though Tati had offered me a ride back home."

"Was there a reason why you declined the ride?"

"Mainly my instinct to decline any offerings like those," he confessed.

"How was the walk home?" Stefanie asked. Liam began to

tentatively stare at Stefanie. Did she know what had happened? How would she even know? She gently laughed a little and put her notepad aside.

"You are probably getting annoyed with me and all these questions, but it's just that I sense that there is something else you haven't mentioned yet," Stefanie clarified.

"You are right. There is something. It was not a good walk home."

"Tell me about it. Was it more flashbacks?" She asked him. His eyes changed their gaze. He looked at his feet shamefully, taking a couple of breaths.

"No. I decided to take a detour, thinking that walking a little longer in the middle of the dark would help ease my mind. Instead, I walked by a group of three men attacking another one. I did nothing. I turned my head and walked away. All I did was call nine one one and deliver an anonymous tip, which wasn't too anonymous since they contacted me back. Anyways turns out the man was stabbed and in critical condition. As of two days ago, he is no longer critical and just recovering," Liam explained. Stefanie moved her hands to adjust her glasses and then made a face after remembering that she wasn't wearing them. It was simply a habit now.

"Interesting. So you feel that the attack was your responsibility?"

"Well, not the attack itself, but allowing the man to be stabbed."

"You didn't know he was going to get stabbed," she challenged him.

"It was like two in the morning or so, three men jumping on another one. Who wouldn't see that it was big trouble?" Liam questioned.

"But you also don't know the full story behind it. Maybe the man isn't so innocent himself. Or Maybe he is. The point is you don't really know it. It is technically not your responsibility. You are trying to live your life as if you do not have superpowers, correct? Without them, you could have been stabbed too and maybe killed."

"But that's the thing, I have the powers. I could have prevented them from doing something terrible."

"If you don't mind me asking, what stopped you? I believe there must have been a reason. There are no wrong answers here," Stefanie reasoned.

"A little over a year ago, I was in a similar situation. Except back then, I didn't turn and walk away. I stepped in. The attacker immediately came at me, so I punched him in the face. The problem was that I didn't quite realize the extent of my strength on a normal person, so while it felt like a simple punch, it ended up being so strong that the man ended up in the hospital. He came so close to dying. The worst part is that he still ended up with permanent brain damage despite not dying. I was afraid of something like that happening again."

"That is understandable. Do you feel like there was anything else you could have done? Maybe just drag them away, and fly over them?" Stefanie wondered.

"Flying would give away my powers. Grabbing them or pushing them away could have been very dangerous too. If I grab them a little too hard, I could crush them. I'm sure they would resist, so I can foresee something terrible happening. Even pushing them away could send one flying against a solid wall and then breaking their back or neck," Liam responded.

"Essentially, you didn't really have any options than to walk away and call nine one one, basically what anyone else would have most likely done. You didn't do anything wrong. If anything, you may have saved the man's life by calling it in. Had you taken a ride with Tati, or if your car had been working, you wouldn't have been able to call the police," Stefanie clarified. Liam leaned back against the couch, resting his right foot on his left knee.

"Huh," he managed to say. Stephanie jotted down a few more notes.

"There is always the opportunity to put different spins into things," she told him.

"I had thought that not even you could find any positive spin into this. I never really thought about it that way."

"Many times, we may not see or think of the easiest possible solutions or spins, especially when it concerns ourselves. People tend to be their own greatest critics," Stefanie elaborated.

"Interesting," Liam managed to say. These sessions continued to surprise him positively. Had he come up with a positive spin on his own, he would have simply dismissed it and said he was just making excuses for himself. He should have never missed that week. Who knows how different things could have been. But instead, he made up his mind that he would not skip any more sessions. It was his only chance to actually be able to challenge himself consistently. He needed the push to forgive himself, something he was beginning to think was possible.

"Do you have anything planned for this week? Any goals?" Stefanie asked him. Worried, Liam quickly checked the time. But, to his relief, he still had half the session remaining.

"I was thinking maybe hang out with Henry and Tati more. Try to look for new ways to keep my mind distracted. For example, when I bought a new sink, it felt great to see a couple so excited while looking for a sink. They had this excitement that I have never personally felt while buying a sink, despite having bought far too many already."

"So people watching seemed to help you out a bit. It looks like that even when you are distant from people, just having people around seems to help with your mind. Have you ever thought about maybe getting a roommate?" Stefanie asked and then studied him for his reactions.

"I... I... I'm not sure. I don't think that may be a good idea. Even if I manage to not hurt him, I don't think I'm ever not going to break a sink ever again. So how could I explain why I break so many sinks?" Liam countered.

"Maybe having someone around would cause you to not break a sink. You've broken nothing at work because you have been able to maintain your guard better."

"Hmm, I would have to think about it. Evaluate all the pros and cons," Liam told her.

"Of course, it shouldn't be a decision you just jump into. It is good food for thought, though," Stefanie elaborated.

"I will definitely be thinking about it, though I'm not entirely sure I will change my mind," Liam admitted.

"That is ok too. At least you will have considered and given it a chance to evaluate. There is no right or wrong answer to it. You just have to keep finding out what works best for you and make the decisions as they seem appropriate," she reiterated to him. Liam nodded; she certainly had made him challenge many of his thoughts, which was good.

"I take it that your sleep still hasn't improved?" Stefanie brought it up.

"No, but it feels like so much keeps on happening. I need to head into a barbershop again soon and shave too. Maybe this coming week. I guess I'll just figure something out to see if I can sleep better."

"Sleeping is significant and would help tremendously with many moods. When we don't get the rest we need, our bodies and minds don't sync well. We also tend to become more prone to feeling down and depressed. So here is an idea, something I will recommend trying out. Even if it doesn't work first, just keep trying. Remove any sort of distractions from your room. Mainly anything related to electronics. If there is something you can't really remove from your room, make sure that it is turned off completely. You could also try getting blackout curtains if you don't already have them. This allows for any outside light to be blocked off. Lay down in your bed an hour before you hope to fall asleep, and then close your eyes and keep them closed as much as possible. Maybe you could try drinking a warm beverage an hour and a half before that time. I know what I'm about to say is really hard, but try to shut down your thoughts as best as possible. If you must, focus on the natural sounds around you. See if any of this helps or works in any way," Stefanie suggested. Liam thought about it for a few seconds and then finally answered.

"Alright. I'll give it a try. I'll keep my phone in the kitchen."

"Good, and remember, don't simply give up if it doesn't work initially. Keep on trying, alright?" Stefanie reinforced.

"Will do, I promise," Liam responded. It was then that he realized their session was close to the end.

"I take it the same day and time next week?" Stefanie asked him while still having a few minutes to spare.

"That will work great," he answered with a smile. Hopefully, he could return the following week with more positive news than this session.

Chapter 14

It had been an hour since Stefanie's last client, but she was still sitting in the room writing down notes. Stefanie again reached for her glasses, forgetting she wasn't wearing them. She shook her head with a smile realizing how silly she must have looked to all her clients throughout the day while attempting to fix her glasses. She closed her notepad and exhaled in relief. Another day had ended, only for it to start over the following day. She would see more clients and find out how their week had gone.

It was a job that probably would only work for some. A big part was listening to what people had to say, watching their reactions and facial expressions, and attempting to decipher emotions that even the clients didn't always realize they had. Some clients were easier to get a good read on than others. Finally, she decided that it was time to call it a night. She grabbed her belongings and then exited the room.

The first thing Stefanie did after she finally arrived home was jump into the shower. After putting in long hours, nothing felt greater than feeling refreshed. When she was finished, she wrapped herself in a tower and allowed her hair to hang wet. Then, she went into her cabinets, took out a popcorn bag, and placed it in the microwave.

While she waited for the popcorn to pop, she grabbed the remote control in the living room and turned on the television. She chose her most used app, where she could either rent or buy digital movies. She started flipping through her choices until she found a few on sale. There was one particular movie that caught her attention. It was based on Faceless. She actually recalled when the film had first come out. It had been such a big deal, yet she had never watched it. She wondered if Liam himself had ever seen it. She decided to purchase the movie out of curiosity. How would they portray Faceless? After all, no one knew who the man behind the mask was. Would they create an entire persona for him? Would Faceless just be faceless the whole movie? How would they give him the powers in the film? So many questions that could only be answered by watching the movie.

The microwave beeped, signaling to Stefanie that the popcorn was ready. She started jogging to the kitchen, where her towel almost fell on the ground. She laughed, remembering she still hadn't put on her pajamas. She walked over to her bedroom and put on her pajamas which she had left on the top of her unmade bed.

She returned to the kitchen, grabbed the popcorn bag, and then walked back to the living room. Then, with her controller, she lay on the couch and moved to the movie, 'The Face of Faceless.'

Couldn't they have come up with a better title? She thought while pressing the start button. Right from the start, she knew the movie would not be great. It was the typical blockbuster movie. They had named him Mark, she felt that it was too generic of a name, but that was nowhere near the worst problem the movie had. It started with him being dumped by a girl who told him she was cheating on him because he was boring.

Stefanie rolled her eyes, cringing at how cheesy the entire scene was. It turns out that Mark was a scientist, and the breakup led to him developing a potion that, in return, gave him superpowers. Stefanie was almost sure that if Liam had seen the movie, he probably would have hated it. Despite hating it from the get-go, Stefanie decided she would still finish the film.

After two and a half hours of what she would refer to as complete and utter bullshit, the movie finally ended. At least they had used the real-life first villain that Liam had fought, even if they got everything about him wrong. After having learned quite a bit from Liam himself and the research she did, it was fair for her to say the whole movie was a terrible fabrication. They had portrayed Mark as someone without flaws after becoming Faceless. Unlike Liam, whose mental state and life had appeared to go downhill after gaining his superpowers, Mark's only went uphill. Although to be fair to the movie makers, they had never claimed it to be the true story.

Stefanie then looked at the time, it was pretty late, and she would have to go to work the following day. She headed to the bathroom and stood in front of her mirror. She stared at it tentatively, seeing how she felt, what she saw. She hoped to better understand Liam's feelings whenever he looked in the mirror. She softly sighed and grabbed her toothbrush. After brushing her teeth, she called it a night and passed out in bed.

The next day came, and like any other day of the week, it would be spent listening to many different people. She didn't spend much time on her hair that morning. Instead, she tied it into a ponytail before leaving her house, but not before making herself a smoothie. Once she was back at the workroom, she took a deep breath, unsure of what to expect from her clients. She could get a lot of positive that day, she could get a lot of negative, or a good mix.

"Tell me about your week," she would start many sessions.

"It was complete and utter shit. I wish a train would have just run me over," one of her clients answered.

"It was fantastic! This girl I really like kissed me on the cheek and said she was interested in me," another client responded. Stefanie would give them her full attention and listen to them. For some people saying the wrong thing could cause extreme harm. Some people may think her job was easy and stress-free, but that was the farthest thing from the truth. You had to understand the people and know how to respond to them in ways where you aren't necessarily lying but not steering them into a route full of false hopes. Her stress was always at a high level. One would never know what could happen within or outside the sessions. Even if the session went exceptionally well, she had no control over how others would act. Some of her clients were just one name-calling away from ending up in another deep depression and regressing backward.

For the most part, her clients had always been great with her. They all trusted her and took her words with high meaning. Even more, reason to be stressed. There had been once when a client had called her a 'fucking bitch,' because she had declined to sleep with him to fulfill one of his lifelong fantasies of sleeping with a shrink. She had vaguely mentioned the story to some friends without saying it had happened to her. Some of the guys thought it was hilarious. She, on the other hand, did not.

She still remembered that day clearly. It had been when she was still relatively new to her job. She had no idea what to expect or how it would end. So when he started yelling at her, she quickly took out her work cell phone. She dialed nine one one without actually pressing the call button. Fortunately for her, he had simply stormed off the room, slamming the door shut, and was never heard from again. Not that she was complaining about the last part.

She waited until the end of the day, only to do it again the following day. Once the weekend arrived, she was relieved and excited. It would be nice to have a few days off, relax, and have time for herself. She slept in a little later than usual that Saturday. She made herself breakfast after waking up. One of her favorite simple breakfast food to make scrambled eggs with sausage and toast. After she finished eating, she went into her car.

She was still determining where she would be heading. All she knew was that she wanted to drive someplace where she could relax and perhaps even do some reading. However, when she pulled out of her parking spot, she was almost hit by a car that was probably going over fifty miles per hour. Her hands began shaking from the rapid scare, and fear soon turned into annoyance. She drove for about thirty minutes before finally reaching a park with an ocean view. *Perfect,* she thought while pulling into a parking spot. She retrieved a chair from the trunk of her car and then found a nice place under a tree. She put her chair down and smiled. She would be able to read there and admire the ocean as well. The weather was finally warming up, which was good despite still being a little chilly.

She opened her book to continue reading where she had left off. She was reading a mystery novel. Those were her favorites. Many people had told her she should start reading audiobooks. She had attempted before but had never gotten into them. What she liked about being out there at that time of the year was that few people were around. It meant things were less noisy, and she was less likely to be bothered by random creeps. Time passed quickly, and when she came to her senses, she had read a good fifty pages of the book. She closed the book and put it inside the bag right by her seat. She checked her personal phone for any new messages and noticed she had been invited out with friends later. She quickly gave them the answer in the group chat and then walked closer to the small wooden logs that separated the road and led to the beach.

Part of her was tempted to walk over to the beach, but a more significant part of her didn't feel like getting any sand on her feet or clothes. There would be plenty of opportunities in the summertime to explore the beach. After taking a few minutes to appreciate the calmness of the water, she grabbed her belongings and returned to her car. She would head home and relax until it was time to meet her friends.

Overall it ended up being a good Saturday for Stefanie. She was able to catch up with a couple of her friends at a restaurant that night, then ended up at a bar dancing alongside her friends. When Sunday came around, she decided it would be a lazy day for her. She watched movie, after movie, after movie. Just like that, Sunday came to an end.

She was back at it again, seeing clients starting early Monday. It was just another regular day that she managed to get through. Tuesday came along without much excitement either, but many of her clients were doing reasonably well for the time being.

By the time Wednesday came, it felt like a very typical week. Listen to the clients and their week, and help drive them in the right direction. She enjoyed her job, and while the routine may look the same, she would hear her clients' stories evolving. She got to see their attitudes change. But, of course, there was also the bad, where she would see them fall again and again.

Wednesday was going just like any other day, that was until her personal phone started ringing when she was alone in the room. She looked at the number, it was no one that was in her contacts. However, she did recognize the area code. It was from the same area her mother lived. Nervously she decided to answer the call.

"Hello, this is Stefanie speaking," she says slowly and nervously.

"Hello, Stefanie. This is Alberta calling on your mother's behalf," the voice responded. The voice was a little deep and a bit coarse as if this woman was an avid smoker. Why would someone be calling on her mother's behalf? That's when Stefanie started to panic and quickly responded.

"Is she alright? Did something happen? Please tell me that she's ok!" She insisted without giving Alberta a chance to speak. There was a bit of silence, which concerned her even more. There were so many thoughts that started running through her mind. She wasn't sure how to feel or what to think. She looked at the time and saw that her last client was scheduled in just a few minutes.

"Relax," Alberta ordered her. *Relax?* Stefanie thought, a little offended. She had no idea who this woman was. Then the first thing she had mentioned was that she was calling on behalf of her mother, and now she told her to relax? Who did she think she was? She remained on the phone and then listened to what Alberta had to say. There was a soft knock on the door. It must have been her last client. As she continued to listen to the call, her face became a little paler, and fear seemed to have struck her.

"Ok... I... I need to work... I will call you back later..." Stefanie told her and then hung up the phone. She took a deep breath and then forced a smile as she approached the door and opened it slowly. On the other side waiting was Liam. His smile was more confident than she was used to seeing.

Andre Pereira

Chapter 15

Stefanie motioned for Liam to walk into the room. She watched him enter and go through his usual routine. First, he looked at the paintings on the wall and sat in the middle of the couch. Her smile faded when she began to have thoughts about her mother again. She stood at the door for a few seconds, almost as if she was frozen, before finally coming to her senses and remembering she was with a client. She forced a smile again and headed back to her seat.

Unlike his other sessions, Liam noticed she didn't even grab her notepad immediately. Instead, he felt as if there was something different about her. It wasn't that she was back to having her glasses on or her hair wasn't straightened like usual. It was just something else. He didn't feel she was as prepared as she usually was. Her energy felt weaker compared to the other times. For some reason, she appeared to be sad. He had always seen a genuine smile from her. Usually, the room was full of positive energy, but this time it simply felt off. He decided he wouldn't bring it up for the time being. Perhaps it was something related to one of her other clients. After all, she was a human being, which meant she was also allowed to have her down days.

"So... tell me about your week," Stefanie finally spoke in a monotone. Liam leaned back against the couch and put his hands together.

"Well, I would say it has been fairly good. I haven't had any extreme panic attacks or visions."

"Oh... That is good... Definitely good..." Stefanie responded, a bit puzzled. She looked like someone who didn't want to be there, even less so listening to someone else's week. Liam was about to ask her if everything was alright, but he decided it would be best not to. Someone like Stefanie would answer with a yes, apologize if things seemed off, and not say anything else about it. So he didn't take it personally. He was much the same way himself to almost anyone else.

"What... what do you think... what do you think made a difference?" She asked him. At first, she stumbled with words, but then she composed herself. Liam raised one of his eyebrows a bit. It was a bit painful seeing someone who is usually so genuine and down to earth the way she currently was.

"Well. I was able to hang out with Tati and Henry again. This

108

time it felt a bit less awkward. As for the other days, I have been going to Mason's Bar. I actually managed to talk some more with Cole himself. He really is a great guy. I also got to meet his wife. She is fairly funny and tough as well. You do not want to get on her bad side. But you can tell how much they love and support each other," Liam answered.

"That's great. You're taking more risks and opportunities, and they are paying off. You are getting more comfortable... That is great progress," Stefanie managed to answer. She looked at Liam, she knew that her heart wasn't in it at that point, and she felt terrible for him. Unfortunately, he was the next person she saw right after her phone call with Alberta. Her mind was in overdrive mode with numerous amounts of questions. What would she do next? How would she handle all of her clients? Luckily for her, Liam appeared to be patient. He gave her some time to think. She sighed, looked at him, and forced a smile, which Liam quickly picked up on.

"I tried doing what you told me to sleep. It helped a little, but my issue has never been electronics or lights. It has always been my thoughts, my mind, and the flashes of the past," Liam added.

"I'm sorry," Stefanie slowly answered. Liam lifted an eyebrow again, confused.

"You don't have to be sorry. You were trying to help. I'm the difficult one. You have been right about everything so far. As I started getting myself out more in the company of others, my mind has been able to soothe a bit. Maybe I'll just never be able to get rid of the nightmares, but maybe I can distract myself a bit better," he admitted. The room went into complete silence again, and Liam's foot slowly tapped the floor. He stood up and started to walk towards the paintings. He was giving Stefanie a few more minutes of quietness.

"Something seems to be bothering you," Liam spoke softly as he stood before a painting. He never looked at her. He hated people staring at him when things were not going great.

"I can tell something must have happened recently. You don't seem like yourself at all," he continued. Stefanie lifted her head and looked in his direction. She sighed before she responded.

"I'm sorry. Right before our session, I got a call from one of my mother's neighbors."
"Everything alright with her?"
"Well, it's not like it's life-threatening, at least not yet, but she

will need surgery. The neighbor told me that the surgery isn't dangerous," Stefanie explained.

"At least that's a good thing."

"I still worry, though, never know when the smallest thing can go wrong in a surgery."

"The doctors will probably do great, but there is nothing wrong with worrying. It is your mother, after all. It would probably be weirder if you were not concerned," Liam counseled. Stefanie let out a weak laugh. Liam turned around, confused.

"Looks like I'm the one in therapy today. Almost like the shoes have been switched," Stefanie joked.

"Ha!" Liam laughed while walking back to the couch. He took a seat and looked at Stefanie. She forced a smile. This time despite it still being weak, it was genuine.

"I'm so sorry, Liam. You are probably not going to be a fan of what I'm going to say next," she told him. This time, he was the one that forced a fake smile.

"You're leaving, aren't you?" He added.

"Not permanently, no. I will still be here for next week's session, but that will be the last for a minimum of a month. I was told that my mother will need someone to help her out after surgery for about a month, potentially longer," Stefanie explained to him.

Liam swallowed his own saliva. He had anticipated that this day might come at some point, yet facing it, in reality, did not feel good. His heart felt like it would explode, and he held back tears of pain and forced himself to speak.

"I understand. Your mother needs you. You need to be there for her," he encouraged. He started rubbing his left eyebrow with his left hand. He attempted to smile a few times, but his cheeks seemed to spasm as he tried. Despite how hard he was trying to hide his disappointment from Stefanie, she could see it. After all, she had made it a career picking up on these things.

"I'll be back, Liam. I'm not moving away permanently. Usually, if I need to go away for that long, I would offer video sessions, but honestly, I'm unsure if I will have the time for them. Even if I did, I think you need to actually be physically present for the sessions. There is nothing wrong with that, but I might have a solution," she spoke softly and empathetically.

"I'm... I'm sorry. I didn't mean to look like an ass. I completely understand that you need to go. I think it's just an initial shock. You have been so great, so understanding and caring. I always look forward to Wednesdays," Liam explained.

"You are stronger and better than you give yourself credit for. Make sure you keep working on the re-framing and getting yourself out there. You're a good person. I was thinking, I know a friend who has been doing this longer than I have. Perhaps you can see her while I'm away. Then, when I return, if you like her better, you can stay with her, and if you want to come back to me, then the spot will still be there," she suggests. Stefanie allows Liam to think for a few seconds, and she figures him to be contemplating the decision. He finally looks up at her and attempts to smile but fails.

"I think it might be good if I at least keep seeing someone. Though I will one hundred percent be back to you once you return," he told Stefanie honestly.

"Well, give her a chance. As I said, she has been doing this longer than I have. Maybe she'll end up being better. I can't promise she has any open spots, she gets a lot of clients, but if she does, I'll make sure to convince her to give it to you. That said, I would like your permission to talk to her about our sessions and pass her my notes. You and I still have next week together, but I want your permission now. I would never ever give out any info without your permission."

"It's ok, you can talk to her about it. She would find out about it anyways in our first session. So might as well make sure she's caught up," Liam responded, still saddened.

"Remember, Liam, you have made so much progress in just about two months, don't let it slip away. I believe in you," Stefanie added.

"What's your friend's name, if you don't mind me asking?"

"Catherine. She has a different personality than me, but that isn't a bad thing. Every client loves her. She's got nothing but positive reviews," Stefanie continued to clarify.

"I trust you," Liam admitted. She noticed that Liam was still looking heartbroken. Despite still having her own concerns, she decided that she still needed to do her job and, for the time being, decided not to think about her mother.

"Anything else happened throughout the week?" She quickly asked him.

"I was waiting for a phone call or visit that I never got," he told her softly without much motivation.

"Phone call or visit?" Stefanie asked, confused. She leaned forward on the chair while adjusting her glasses and then laid back against the chair.

"Yeah, the police had called me, related to my phone call. I wasn't exactly a kiss butt, so to speak.

"You didn't do anything wrong, so they can call all they want, but they won't be able to do anything else."

"We'll see. The officer that spoke with me on the phone seemed to throw implications," Liam answered.

"He was probably trying to instill fear, hoping you'd end up letting something slip," Stefanie suggested. Liam then looked at his hands, both playing with one another.

"Does your mother live far away?" He finally managed to ask.

"It's about a two-hour flight," she responded to him.

"I know I've mentioned it today, but coming here was my best decision. You have been great," Liam told her. He wanted to remain optimistic, but something in him told him he might never see her again after she left. So he forced another soft smile.

"Next week, we can go over goals you want to accomplish while I'm away."

"Sounds good," he replied. They spent the remaining of the session with what felt like small talk. Then, when the time came, he walked out of the room, and as soon as he stepped outside, a harsh reality hit him. He only had one more week to look forward to his session with Stefanie.

Chapter 16

When Liam woke up the following day, it was only five in the morning. He didn't want to get out of bed. He didn't want to do anything. The world felt good enough at that moment, just laying in bed as if nothing else existed. His stomach growled at him, he'd not eaten anything since before he had seen Stefanie the previous evening, but he did not care.

Was this how life was going to become once she went away? He knew he shouldn't be feeling that way. It was not like he would stop having sessions; they'd simply be with someone new. *New*, he thought. Getting him to his first session with Stefanie had already been tough enough. He wasn't a fan of new. It always made him feel stressed and anxious. What if she couldn't handle his resistance and told him to leave immediately? What if she laughed at him and told him he was a liar. What if she made him have to prove he had powers? Something Stefanie had never really bothered to question if he was honest or not.

Couldn't entirely blame anyone if they ever doubted that he was telling the truth about his superpowers. What reason would he have to lie anyways? There were so many questions he didn't want to even think about anything at all. Yet, that too, was not possible. He knew he had to go to work later. There was no way he could miss any more time at work due to self-pettiness. The next time he checked, the time was at nine-thirty in the morning, and his stomach was growling at him more than ever.

Fine, I'll eat. He reluctantly got himself out of bed and headed to the kitchen. He took out a muffin and placed it on the toaster. He watched the toaster as if anything interesting was about to happen. Frozen at the moment until it popped. He took it out and, without thinking, started eating them as they were. He walked back to his bed, where he laid back down.

Ha, ha, such a loser. You should have known that Stefanie would also disappear from your life.

Why can't you just shut up?

Poor wittle Liam, can't he handle his own mind.

Liam quickly turned to the side, grabbed a pillow, and pressed it against his face as if it would help shut down his inner voice. Time continued to tick away until it was time to go to work.

113

Once he made it to work, he paid no attention to Josh, who had already started to walk towards him, no doubt to complain about something. Instead, Liam managed to dodge him altogether. He tried as hard as he could to stay away from everyone, and when Josh finally caught up to him, Liam lied and told Josh that his stomach wasn't feeling well.

"Oh shit, you stay away from me. The last thing I need is the shitters," Josh remarked while walking away. Perhaps he should have done this plenty of other times had he known how easy it would have kept Josh away. Nevertheless, he managed to get through the first half of his shift. During lunch, he sat quietly in his car as usual. His eyes were open, but his mind was elsewhere. He jumped as soon as someone knocked on the window of the driver's side. He turned his head to see Henry standing there. He pressed a button, and his window slid down.

"Are you alright? You seem like you lost a lot of that energy from last week," Henry pointed out. Liam then looked back to his steering wheel.

"Yeah, I'm fine. Just silly stuff. I'll get over it," Liam answered, unsure how much he actually meant it.

"Alright. Well, if you do need someone to talk to, feel free to reach out anytime," Henry offered. Liam nodded and then looked at Henry and forced a smile.

"Thank you. I appreciate it," Liam affirmed. Henry smiled before leaving him alone again. That pretty much summed up the remainder of his day. He finished his work, but his mind had wandered to different places for most of his shift. So it was a relief when the time came to clock out.

Rather than going straight home, he stopped by Mason's Bar. He sat at his usual spot at the counter and waited for the bartender. To his disappointment, neither Cole nor his wife were there that day. Instead, it was a bartender he'd not yet met. He asked for a Shirley Temple, which he had grown fond of. He drank it rather quickly and then left and ensured to leave back a good tip. He had overheard a couple of men critiquing his choice of drink. Still, he had decided to ignore it and not let it upset him further.

He was forced to park his car several blocks away from his apartment. Someone must have been having a big sleepover or having some sort of gathering. Rather strange for a Thursday, but then again, life was weird. Once he returned to his house, he walked towards the living room. He was about to pick up the journal lying on that couch untouched. 'Nah,' he decided against it going crazy as he attempted to figure out what he was in the mood for. He shook his head some more and then headed to the bathroom.

There was a brand new mirror. He had finally replaced it the day before he went to see Stefanie. He had started to feel himself get more comfortable in his own skin and had even been able to look in the mirror. However, he could not look at it again at that particular point. He knew exactly what he would find if he looked. He would see disgust, hatred, anger, and a pathetic person everyone decided to disappear from. He grabbed his toothbrush and began to brush his teeth to a classical song he had put on his cell phone.

Once he finished in the bathroom, he went straight to the kitchen and filled a cup with some water. He went to his refrigerator, grabbed an English muffin, and ate it cold. The first time he had actually eaten anything the whole entire day. Once done eating, he went and dove into bed with his stomach face down, skipping his usual shower routine. He closed his eyes and the struggle would start.

He tried to counter his thoughts and lock them away, but it was not working. Things he'd been trying not to think about for the entire week started to return to his mind. '*You killed my mommyyy,*' the haunting voice of a child returned to his head. The voice repeated the exact words until he could not bear it any longer and screamed really loud. He jumped out of bed, and as he did, he checked the time, a little past one in the morning. He quickly jogged to the bathroom and turned the shower on to his usual setting. He started to wonder if his neighbors had heard him scream, and if so would they say anything about it? Who was he kidding? Of course, they had heard him. If anything, they must have grown used to it by now. What a joke, a grown man constantly losing his mind.

Once the water was hot enough, he filled the tub before undressing and stepping in. He laid down inside the tub, his entire body except his head submerged. He closed his eyes and started taking deep breaths. "Inhale.... exhale," he would softly tell himself. "Breath in... breath out.... breath in... breath out...." Liam continued. Slowly his entire world disappeared, and he now stood in a complete void. There was no stress, no noise, no clutter. Just an endless void of nothing. *Breathe in...*

breathe out... breathe in... breathe out...

'YOU KILLED MY MOMMYYYY,' Liam immediately shook in the tub. Without opening his eyes, this was the loudest the voice had ever felt in his mind.

'No! Stop!' Liam yelled out in the void.

'YOU KILLED MY MOMMYYYY,' the child's voice yelled again. It felt like it was getting closer to him. It was definitely coming from behind him, so he started to run as fast as he possibly could, hoping that the child's voice wouldn't be able to keep up with him. Somehow, he felt as if no progress was being made. It was hard to tell; everything looked identical in the void. *Breath in, breath out, breath in, breath out,* his breaths hastened, and his heart went from a constant soft beat to irregular consecutive quick beats. Boom, boom, boom, boom. Liam began twitching and turning in the bathtub, water splashing everywhere. The void turned into an area surrounded by countless dead bodies. In any direction he looked, there were mountains of dead bodies, and right in front of him was a child's silhouette.

'You killed my mommy,' the child spoke softly. The child raised a finger and pointed it towards Liam, who stood there frozen, gasping for air while his panic increased. Tears started trickling down Liam's face in torment and emotional pain. He looked at the child and dropped to his knees, crying.

'I'm so sorry... I di... I didn't mean to... It wasn't supposed to have gone that way. Tanner... Tanner wouldn't let me steer him away.' Liam tried to explain, barely able to breathe and with a sharp pain in his heart that continued to grow.

'Excuses! It is all your fault... It was all you!" The child told him menacingly. Liam bowed his head down while putting both hands on his forehead, crying more than ever.

He came to his senses when he heard a few strong knocks on his door. He quickly got up from the tub and noticed the water that he had splashed everywhere. He grabbed a towel and wrapped it around himself. He looked at his cell phone and saw it was now a few minutes past two.

He answered the door and saw that it was his neighbor from downstairs. The man was thin like a stick, with barely any hair except for a few short strands. It would have been this man if stick figures had been based on anyone. He did not seem amused, and Liam wasn't sure if it was because he had only wrapped himself in a towel or if he'd been making too much noise.

"What is going on over here? We try to sleep downstairs, and what? You having playtime over here?" The man angrily told him.

"I'm sorry," Liam managed to say, embarrassed.

"Look, we hear a lot of weird shit coming from this house that we ignore because it's really not my business as to whatever kinky shit you are into. But come on, man, not during the night," the man warned him.

"I understand, and you are right. I am very sorry," was all Liam was able to muster.

"Ok, good. I will just tell my wife you were having a bad dream," the man attempted to joke, yet Liam could not find it funny. He closed the door as the man walked back downstairs. His heart still felt like it was racing the fastest person in the world. He raised his hands to his eye level and observed them as they shook uncontrollably. He returned to the bathroom and decided to let the tub drain out. He returned to his bedroom holding his clothes and then put them on again. He threw himself into bed one more time.

That wasn't the only day things seemed to hit a rough patch. His mood didn't quite get any better during the following days. He kept himself in solitude, minding his own business. He skipped his general trips to Mason's Bar and went straight home instead. He tried upping the dosage of melatonin. As always, it didn't work for him.

He made sure his showers remained just showers rather than baths. His flashes were starting to return more frequently. As each day came and went, he was closer to being on his last session with Stefanie, or as she would tell him, just temporarily.

Tuesday came around, and he was determined to try and get himself into a better state of mind. He did not wish to see Stefanie the following day and only had news of relapsing instead of taking her advice. He woke up and tried to fool himself into thinking that the day would be great. Like most days at work, he kept to himself, but this time he decided to join Henry and Tati on lunch break rather than heading to his car alone. Josh was off that day, which also helped make the day smoother.

Once he left work, he returned to his house to shower quickly and change into jeans and a shirt. He then drove back to Mason's bar. It was pretty empty, despite being karaoke night. He walked inside and took a seat by the bar. The bartender on that night was Cole himself, who, as soon as he saw Liam grabbed an empty glass and made Liam a Shirley Temple. He put it right before Liam and took his card to start a tab.

"How are you doing tonight?" Cole asked with his usual confidence and assertiveness.

"Just another day, that's all," Liam casually responded.

"Thanks for not being typical and saying another day in paradise," Cole joked.

"I don't think I would ever go that far."

"You can't possibly imagine how many people come here and say, another day in paradise. Either drop the paradise or just come up with something new entirely," Cole mentioned. Liam raised his glass and drank through the straw. He gently placed it back on top of the coaster before letting out a small laugh.

"I can see how it would get tiring hearing the same thing repeatedly," Liam mentioned.

"Have I told you the wife and myself are going out of town next week, taking a vacation," Cole mentioned.

"Oh really? That's great! Where are you going?"

"We will be taking a trip to Hawaii. We are very excited. We haven't taken a vacation in such a long time. I'm leaving Thelma in charge for the week. She is the only one I can trust to do so anyways," Cole told him. Liam began thinking for a bit.

"Have I met Thelma?" He asked.

"Probably not. She usually works during the day, though she will work extra hours next week to ensure the bar doesn't collapse. She's excited about it. She likes the responsibility, especially since she wants to move up in the world," Cole told him. The remainder of the night went pretty quietly. Karaoke had been canceled since the person that usually ran it couldn't make it. A couple of other people had sat by the bar, made some small talk, and then left. When one in the morning came around, and the bar closed, Liam was quickly reminded that the following day he had an appointment with Stefanie.

Chapter 17

Liam walked inside the main building, mentally preparing himself. He went up a flight of stairs and gently knocked on the door. He waited a few seconds, and then the door opened. Stefanie appeared to be in a better mood than the previous week. Of course, she did the last time she had gotten the call just before seeing him. She probably had assessed the situation and planned everything out by now. Liam walked inside, knowing it would be at least a month before the next time he'd walk into this room. He looked at the paintings one more time. He wondered if Catherine would also have exciting images for him to appreciate, study, and distract himself with.

"Unfortunately, Catherine is not as much a fan of paintings as I am," Stefanie pointed out, almost as if she had read his mind.

"How do you know I was thinking about that?" Liam asked, puzzled.

"I didn't really. It's just that you like looking at the paintings every time you come in. Just wanted to prepare you."

"I take it she said yes, then?" Liam asked.

"She did. You'll have to see her a couple of hours later on Wednesday. Over here, you come at five. It'll be at seven with her," Stefanie explained while sitting on her usual chair. Liam noticed she had cleaned up several notepads and notebooks from the stand beside it. She probably didn't want to chance leaving them there; maybe something would happen, and she wouldn't be back.

"What if you decide not to return?" Liam asked.

"I'll return. I didn't just buy a house a year ago to abandon it," Stefanie gently replied. Liam nodded and then gazed around the room, attempting to spot anything new or something he may have missed in the last couple of months.

"I had a night out with Catherine. Went over all of our sessions and gave her my notes. Well, I photocopied my notepad. I'll keep that if you decide to return when I return."

"Of course I will," Liam answered.

"I also gave her all your info, including insurance."

"Thank you," Liam told her.

"No, thank you for giving me permission to do so. It'll make it much easier for when you start seeing her next Wednesday. So don't forget next week, at seven at night. I'll also give you the address. Her office is in a much fancier-looking building than mine."

"This one is perfect," Liam admitted.

"Thank you. As I have told you before, her name is Catherine. She is very different from myself. It's either that she has more energy or is just a lot more talkative than I am. The best way for me to put it is that if we were at a party, she would probably be the wild one," Stefanie told him. After taking a second, she quickly spoke again.

"By that, I mean in the most positive way possible," she clarified. Liam managed to smile.

"I understand. Thank you for doing all that for me. You didn't have to. Could have just told me to figure it out on my own," he told her.

"I could never do that to anyone. I am the one who is abruptly leaving. I want to ensure all my clients are well taken care of."

"Is Catherine taking all of your clients?" Liam asked curiously.

"Oh gosh, no. She has too many clients to be able to take that many. I didn't even try to get her to take anyone else. No, you're the only one going to Catherine. Some clients are okay about going a month or potentially a little longer without any sessions. Others said they already had someone else in mind, while others I directed them to other counselors," Stefanie explained to him.

"That is really nice of you. To do all of that for your clients. It proves that you are very dedicated and much more than that. That you are a kind human being," Liam assured her. Stefanie smiled with a hint of blushing a little as she leaned back against her chair. It was time to get going with the session.

"So, tell me about your week. I feel like last week I failed you, and I am very sorry for that."

"Don't be sorry. You're as much human as anyone else. Like everyone else, you are allowed to have off days, months, whatever time you need," Liam quickly responded. Stefanie laughed and nodded.

"Looks like I'm the one having therapy tonight," she joked.

"I doubt you need it. As for my week, it was quite the ride. I had another panic attack at one point in my house. Regressed back quite a bit, though I think I pulled myself together as of yesterday again."

"Regressed back, you say? What does that mean exactly?" Stefanie asked while she grabbed her notepad and started writing down notes.

"I started having flashbacks again, hearing the voices and screams in my head. My mood shifted. I started to feel more gloomy all the time. I wasn't going to Mason's bar. I stayed away from Henry and Tati," Liam responded while Stefanie observed him.

"What do you think prompted the flashbacks coming back?" She curiously asked. Liam looked at her briefly, rubbing his chin while carefully thinking. Did he want to admit that her news of going away had shifted his mood into one big panic attack? No. It wasn't the right thing to do. He couldn't do that to her. It wasn't her fault, and she should not feel guilty about it.

"Weakness on my part. I let everything I learned here slip away. You know, everything I've come to learn about myself," Liam told her. It was basically the condensed truth.

"Did something happen that caused you to forget all of that?" Stefanie asked him. She gave him half a smile. Liam started feeling she probably knew the real reason but wanted him to tell her. *I'm not that brave,* he thought as he smiled back at her.

"Honestly, I don't know. Maybe I got too comfortable and wasn't thinking about how easy it could be to revert to before."

"Are you scared it will be an issue while I'm gone?" Stefanie asked him while jotting down a few more notes.

"Maybe a little. But I'm sure Catherine will be able to help me out," Liam sort of lied. The truth was, he had no idea who Catherine was or what she was like. All he could go on was Stefanie's words, but he didn't want to feel cruel towards her. He gazed at her hand as she jotted down a few more notes.

"You know, I always imagine that all the notes you take would just end up being all doodles and stick figures," Liam joked. Stefanie started laughing and then put the notepad on her legs.

"That would be quite funny. I assure you that isn't what I'm doing," she answered.

"I know. It's just one of those funny thoughts that I sometimes think about," Liam told her.

"As long as it's a positive thought and not a negative reinforcement," Stefanie clarified.

"Of course, it's good. Do you usually fly to go see your mother?" Liam curiously asked.

"Sometimes, other times, I like to drive and take the road trip," she answered.

"I've always liked the idea of a long road trip. Maybe one day I will take one. Experience life from a different lens," Liam spoke while daydreaming. Stefanie had an intrigued look as she jotted down a few more things.

"It's hard for me to accept that this is our last session for a month or more. I've really looked forward to coming here week after week. I feel like I can be candid and not get judged."

"Before our session ends today, we will review your goals while I am away. Please do the best you can with them. Failing isn't wrong, either. Remember the moments you've had recently that made you feel better. Those moments can help you from regressing. You're a better person than you give yourself for," Stefanie surmised while quickly adjusting her glasses. Before Liam had another chance to speak, she interjected.

"I think that no matter how long it takes, one of the ultimate goals is to get you to look in the mirror and smile. I don't think it should be your goal while I'm away, but down the line, and the rest is prepping you up for it," she explained. He nodded at her while standing up and approaching the paintings again. He didn't know when he would get a chance to see the paintings again, so he wanted one last look at it.

"I bought a new mirror and was able to look at it for a couple days, but now I'm back to not looking at it," he confessed.

"It's still progress," she kindly answered. She then watched him for a little bit in front of the paintings.

"Take the painting with you. Bring it up to our first session once I return. If you decide to stay with Catherine, you can bring it back or keep it," Stefanie stated. Liam turned around, moved by the thought. He then looked at the painting again and then at Stefanie.

"I... I couldn't... it's yours," he stumbled on words.

"It's ok. Maybe it'll keep some familiarity while I am gone," Stefanie added. He then looked at the painting again; it was the one where everyone appeared to be pointing to one person in particular.

"Alright, I'll do it. I promise to bring it back, though," Liam assured her. She smiled and watched him take the painting from the wall and bring it to the couch.

"Let's discuss your goals," Stefanie brought it up. Liam carefully placed the painting right next to him and then took a couple of deep breaths.

"To continue to take what you taught me and continue to apply it in my everyday life."

"What exactly are those things that I thought you?" Stefanie challenged.

"That I am not as worthless or as bad as I make myself to be. To re-frame negative thoughts into positive ones. Just because my first instinct is always a negative idea, it does not make it true," he answered confidently.

"Good. What other goals do you have?" She asked as if trying to challenge him even further.

"To continue to put myself around people, specifically those with positive attitudes," Liam added. He paused and thought for a few seconds before speaking again.

"Break less bathroom sinks too. That would be nice. I bet I could have a big savings account if I hadn't broken so many already," he joked. Stefanie laughed while deciding to play along.

"If you wanted to stop breaking sinks, what could possibly help that out?"

"Maybe I can find something cheaper to constantly punch and let out some built-in aggression; maybe that'll help me from taking it out on the sink," Liam softly responded, almost as if he'd just made a discovery.

"That must be it! Built-in aggression keeps being taken out on the sink," he notified Stefanie. She looked at him with a smile bigger than he had ever seen.

"See! You're challenging yourself, making brand new realizations. This is good. This is what I want you to keep doing while I am away. I think you got this," she encouraged him.

"You are brilliant. I'll definitely miss you while you are gone," Liam reiterated. She smiled and jotted down a few more notes. Each passing second meant a moment closer to the end of their session.

"I want you to know that you are awesome at your job, and I'm glad I took the plunge and came. Truth is, when I reached the first door to the building, I almost turned back as I held the handle. However, something in my mind decided to just push me in and do it. Glad I did. I hope everything goes smoothly with your mother's surgery," Liam explained.

"Thank you for trusting me. It can be difficult to admit to a secret as big as yours, but you took a chance with me. I also learned a different side to having superpowers that you never see in the movies, the emotional consequences," Stefanie answered. Liam smiled and then looked at the time. It was almost done. Usually, they would plan the following week, but not this time. Instead, she reminded him that he would meet with Catherine at seven P.M. the next Wednesday and handed him a card with the address.

"Remember, she will be different from myself, but she's outstanding and has been at it longer than I have. I think she will help you a lot as well," she reiterated to him. He gave her a fake smile, one he desperately wanted to believe was real, yet he was filled with false hope.

"Did you get to pack yet?" Liam asked her casually as he stood up, glancing at the door but trying to buy as much time as possible.

"Not yet; I'm usually a last-minute packer. I'll probably be stressing myself about it until the very night before I leave," she admitted with a smile as she stood up and walked towards the door. Liam was about to leave before Stefanie reminded him to grab the painting.

Liam nodded, pointed to his head as if he'd forgotten, and returned to the door.

"Liam, take care. I believe in you. You will do great. I will see you in a month or at least close to it," she told him. He nodded and shook her hand.

"Thank you for everything," Liam told her and stepped out of the room. She closed the door behind him, and he turned to look at the door one more time.

Chapter 18

He was now outside the building itself. He looked back at the building, standing at the sidewalk's curb. There were a total of three floors. Liam began to wonder what Catherine's office and building would look like. He had been warned by Stefanie that it was a more fancy building, which had left him curious.

He took another step away from the building and wondered what all its other offices were used for. He recalled seeing names of other companies on the floor map; he wasn't sure which ones, though. Taking another sigh, he crossed the street and headed to his car. He kept swinging the key ring around his finger as he approached his car.

He reached his car, jumped into the driver's seat, and placed the painting on the passenger's side. He put the key in the ignition and slowly turned it. The car started up smoothly, and he began reversing. This would be a long week, no worse, a long month. He had just left his session, and already, his mind was starting to spiral down again. NO! He couldn't allow that. He was only feeling this way because change was always scary for him. Stefanie had endorsed Catherine, meaning he would have to trust her. He couldn't be selfish; she needed to attend to her mother. The most important thing of all was that she was coming back.

He then began to drive away, and rather than going straight home, he decided to simply drive around with no specific destination in mind. He ended up driving himself to a hill. He parked the car and got out. He walked to a small park across the street where he had quite the sight of the capital city. The lights from the tall buildings made it for a stunning scenery. It was mesmerizing to stare at. It gave him a feeling of calmness. Maybe it was that he had never really had a big battle at night, the one time of the day he'd never actually caused any destruction.

He approached the rails that kept people from falling into a lower street. A couple on the bench were smoking a blunt as he walked past them. He wasn't a fan of the smell. Down to his right, someone appeared to be modeling and taking pictures. *Terrible lighting for pictures. They certainly weren't going to look professional.* He thought, but then again, what did he know about professional photography? A few more people were around, but none were paying attention to him, which he liked. He'd been told by many that it could be easy to run into trouble at night in that particular spot. The experience was far different than what people had claimed. It made him question if they were the ones who would look for trouble. He returned to his car and decided to head back home.

Once home, he sat on his couch and grabbed his remote control. He turned on the television and then picked one of the applications on it to put some music playing. He was going to attempt to start a new routine. Maybe it would stick, perhaps it would die out in a few days; what did it matter anyway? He had to live in the present, not in the future.

He got on the floor and started doing as many push-ups as possible. Once he finished with them, he changed over to crunches. From there, he kept changing the workout, mixing in stretching. He spent a good hour before stopping and grabbing some water. He wasn't sweating or even out of breath; his mind seemed to be running with far more energy than it had in a while. Indeed, it wouldn't help him fall asleep anytime soon, but at least mentally, he was more elevated than usual.

Liam filled up his bathtub, where he could lay in it and relax for a good hour. His mind attempted to sidetrack itself into darker thoughts, but he refused to allow it for the night. He wasn't going to let it ruin his night. Instead of closing his eyes, he simply kept them open and relaxed. Rather than allowing his mind to take over his thoughts, he came up with thoughts himself. Some thoughts made sense, some didn't make any sense.

He was able to make it through the night, even going so far as getting five hours of sleep. The next day, he felt refreshed as he prepared for work. Nothing was thoroughly planned for after work, but Mason's Bar would always be there if nothing else came up. He left his house early and took a few detours to work rather than his usual direct route. He spotted Josh and Mike smoking as usual when he parked his car. Rather than leaving his car and heading inside, Liam remained a little longer, wanting to avoid Josh and Mike's mouths. The two had been making a lot of snarky remarks lately precisely because Liam had been spending more time with Henry and Tati.

He saw them staring at his car and talking from his rearview mirror. He had no doubt it was about him. He noted that he did not care. It was their problem and not his. He noticed Josh pointing straight to his car. Liam tensed up but decided to go back and tell himself again that it was not his problem but theirs.

He kept watching the time on his car radio, hoping they would just go inside, but they didn't. They didn't look like they were talking anymore, standing there and staring at Liam's car.

Fuck faces. He thought as he started to feel his muscles tensing up in anger. He grabbed his steering wheel and held to it softly while he began to take a few deep breaths with his eyes closed. By the time he opened his eyes, they were still there, with just one minute until his starting time. Infuriated, he turned off the engine of his car and walked outside. After making sure the car was locked, he started to walk towards the building without taking as much as one glance at Josh and Mike.

"Oh look, it's mister too good to talk to us now," Josh spat out.

"I just prefer to focus on work," Liam responded without looking at them.

"Yeah, sure, with the fucking weirdos, am I right?" Josh quickly replied. Liam knew who he was talking about reasonably well, and he certainly didn't appreciate the name-calling. However, he knew shaking his head and walking inside would be best. He didn't hear anything else from Josh for the remainder of his shift. Still, he constantly spotted Josh staring in his direction, whispering to Mike and even Chazz. When his shift ended, he quickly found himself back in his car. By then, Liam was entirely aggravated. He turned on the engine and drove away a little faster than he had intended to. He slammed his car door, nearly breaking it, and went inside his house.

I could punch them once in the face, and they would never be able to talk again.

Chill, Liam, chill. Anger isn't the way.

Maybe that's what some people need!

No, no, no. I can't think this way. I'll be disappointing Stefanie.

Control yourself, Liam, control yourself!

Liam ran the water on the bathroom sink and splashed his face a few times with it. He couldn't stay in his house for the remainder of the night. If he did, he would probably have to search for another sink the following day. After showering and getting ready, he drove himself to Mason's Bar. Still, before he pulled into the parking lot, he noticed that Josh and Mike were outside smoking. Rather than pulling into the parking lot, he continued to drive away.

Pieces of shit already ruined my day, and now they want to ruin my night as well! Liam's foot angrily pressed on the gas pedal. His car sped up until he had to turn to get on the highway. Once he reached the highway, he started to speed up again. He drove for about twenty minutes and made it to a small beach. A place he once used to come to just sit in his car and relax while watching the water in front of him. By the time he made it there, there was a police car blocking the entrance to the parking lot. The officer rolled down his window and gestured for Liam to turn around and drive away.

"Why?" Liam asked, feeling frustrated.

"Closed for the night," the officer responded with an attitude.

"Really? We live on a planet where we can't even enjoy its natural aspects at any time? This is some bullshit," Liam shouted loudly as he pressed the button to raise his window up again. He turned his car before he'd give the officer any more reason to provide him with tickets. He started driving away, lost in his head, with no idea where to go. He drove back onto the highway, heading towards home. Tears started coming down his eyes, feeling defeated and unable to control his emotions anymore.

Fuck this! He thought as he took the first exit he saw and started driving someplace he was not familiar with. He parked on the street somewhere, reclined his seat, and laid back against it. He began to take quick and heavy breaths; his lungs felt tight, and his heart was beating the way it always did when he entered into a panic frenzy. His hands shook uncontrollably, and sweat poured down his face.

Why it's so damn hot? Why it's so damn cold? His mind was racing, and he once again doubted himself capable of heeding Stefanie's advice.

I'm so sorry! I tried... I really tried... I don't know if I can. More tears started to come down his face. It felt like a never ending cycle. Would there ever be an end to this cycle? Or would it just continue to reoccur until the end of time? Until he got old? *Shit!* Would he get old? That was an entirely different side of his powers that he didn't even know how it worked. Ever since obtaining them, he had never once been sick. Did that mean he wouldn't age like everyone else, either? Why had he never thought about that before? This could be an entirely new problem he'd never considered. Did he look older than when he'd gotten his powers seven years prior? He had no idea. Even other people he'd known seven years prior still looked the same to him.

He trembled when there was a knock on the window of the

passenger's side. There was a light flashing right into it. He looked to see a police officer holding up a flashlight. He quickly returned the seat and pressed a button to lower the window.

"What is going on over here?" The officer casually asked. The man looked young, most likely mid-twenties. His partner was probably watching from either inside the car or somewhere not far from him. *Great, this guy will try to prove he has big balls.* Liam thought while he took a couple of seconds to respond.

"I'm just trying to relax my mind," Liam told him. Immediately regretting it. It wouldn't be hard for it to be taken out of context.

"Relaxing your mind from what?" The officer asked. *Great.* Just as Liam had expected, the officer had caught it.

"Stressful day of work."

"Oh yeah? What do you do for work?" What was it with officers and not letting anything slide by with Liam? First, the anonymous call he'd made, now just sitting in his car, bothering no one.

"I'm sorry, officer. Have I done anything illegal?"

"I don't know. You tell me." Liam looked away from the officer, his frustrations growing. *This little shit really is trying to stir something up.*

"You're the man of law and order. You tell me," Liam replied back with a bit of sass. *I'm going to prison.* The officer turned off the flashlight and took a step back.

"You are parked here in the middle of the night with your engine running."

"It is a parking space. Is there a curfew I broke or something? Why is it bad that I park here in the middle of the night, and yet if it was the middle of the day, you would pay no attention to me?" Liam added. He didn't know why, but he was feeling fierce and confident out of nowhere. Perhaps it was the adrenaline running through him, enhanced by his recent frustrations, but he thought he was untouchable. Then he realized that he should probably tone it down before things did escalate. The last thing that he would want to happen was to get involved in something and lose control of himself.

"I'm sorry, officer. Like I said, it's been a long, stressful day at work," Liam added with a softer tone.

"What do you do for work?" The officer asked.

"I load trucks. That's what I do. Nothing that exciting," Liam answered.

"I'll let you go. Make sure you think about how you can make yourself look suspicious. Just being parked here with your headlights on and engine running too long," the officer answered.

"Yes, sir," Liam replied. He heard the officer's step walking away from the car and then overheard him talking to his partner.

"I didn't smell any weed or alcohol. Think he just had a bad day." Liam made sure his window came back up fully. Privileged, lucky, that's how Liam felt at that point. He put his blinker on and began driving away. It was time to go home and rethink his entire day and how he had allowed his emotions to get the best of him.

Chapter 19

The time had come for his first session with Catherine. He now stood outside a building that had recently been renovated. The paint job looked fresh, and the lawn was fully decorated and well cared for. He went up the steps and approached the main door. His hands were shaking as he reached for the handle. His heart was quickly beating while opening the door. He then carefully stepped inside.

There was a strong smell of something tropical. It was a good and fresh smell. Liam had never been to Hawaii, but he would imagine it smelled like this. Unlike Stefanie's location, where the first thing he would see was a staircase, this was a long corridor with doors on both sides. He took several steps forward, his nerves still getting the best of him as he trembled. He grabbed the phone from his back pocket and looked through it as he walked on. It kept his mind distracted from the surroundings. He wouldn't have to look at anyone if someone walked by.

He heard a door close and steps walking out of a room, but he didn't dare look. No, this felt like one of the scariest things he had ever done. While he walked forward, someone was walking towards him, but Liam never glanced. His eyes remained fixated on his phone. It felt that the person had paused for a few seconds to stare at him, but then again, he was probably just getting paranoid.

He heard the person, whoever they were, reach the end and exit the building. He then looked up and found the number that belonged to Catherine's room. Should he knock? Or should he wait? Why had no one ever trained him for this situation? He decided to knock; what's the worst that could happen? Well, she could tell him how big of a failure and loser he was and send him away immediately. In which case, she would notify Stefanie how he couldn't even just wait and was needy, and Stefanie, too, would drop him. *Just excuses you tell yourself, Liam.*

Right.

Liam gently knocked twice on the door and took a few steps away. He waited until he finally saw the door open. Standing there was a woman with a big smile, showing her perfectly shaped white teeth. She had curly brown hair down her shoulders and wore a skirt down to her knees. She was also wearing a red headband.

"You must be Liam!" She spoke with a lot of energy and personality. She moved from the door and stretched her arm as if telling

Liam to walk inside.

"Yes, I am," he responded, gently bowing his head and entering the room. There was a strong smell of perfume as he walked by her. The room itself smelled pretty nice, too. Much like the hallway, it was like a tropical smell, a tropical fruity juice. Unlike Stefanie, she had no paintings on the wall. Instead, it had a number in one spot made of metal and nothing else. He stared around the office; it felt very minimalist. It was probably her style.

The room itself was smaller and cozier than Stefanie's. It was definitely much brighter, as well. The couch in the middle was also smaller. Although Stefanie's couch was divided into three spots, it could have easily had four people sitting on it. Yet, this one had two spots and would likely only fit two people. Despite the smaller size, it was still more expensive than Stefanie's. It must have been the extra experience and the fact that she had far more clients than Stefanie.

The chair Catherine sat in was also far more expensive and fancier. It was cushioned on the back and the seat itself. It was beside the couch, with barely any space between them. Liam continued walking towards the sofa, already feeling slightly disappointed that there wasn't much on the walls he could distract himself with.

"Please have a seat; don't be shy," Catherine spoke again as she rushed to one of her stands and grabbed a notebook alongside some papers. Liam nodded without a sound and then took a seat on the couch. Catherine sat on her comfortable chair and gave him a big smile as she went through the loose papers on top of her notebook.

"Unfortunately, despite Stefanie handing me all of her notes, I'm still going to need you to sign some paperwork. The usual boring stuff, privacy, allowing me to contact insurance, blah, blah, blah," she rapidly spoke, filled with energy. Liam nodded. He understood and then grabbed the papers while she handed them to him. He skimmed through them quickly, signed them, then handed them back to Catherine.

"Perfect! Glad that's out of the way. My name is Catherine, as I am sure you already know. Let's see, I love my job; I've been doing it for a few years now. Since I'm only thirty-four, I'm sure I'll be doing it for many more years to come. I love helping people. I want to see the best for my clients and hate seeing them in pain," she revealed with a smile.

"I'm Liam Lewis; I have superpowers," he added slowly and uncomfortably.

"I read through all of Stefanie's notes. We also talked over a few drinks in person, so we don't have to make you go through everything again. So let's see, we can start with your week."

"My week?"

"Yes, how did this week go, knowing that you wouldn't have that comfort of familiarity once Wednesday came?" Catherine pointed out. She was holding a notebook with a hard cover with random designs. She held a pen in her other hand.

"Oh. Well... It's been a struggle... Haven't done a very good job at controlling my emotions," Liam admitted, embarrassed.

"Interesting. Would you like to elaborate on that?" She curiously asked while leaning forward on her chair.

"Well, I... umm... I was getting angry at every little thing. This guy at work who is always so annoying..."

"Would that be Josh?" Catherine interrupted him. Liam looked up, puzzled, and noticed Catherine smiling at him.

"Don't be so surprised. I told you I spoke with Stefanie and read her notes. She writes a lot of important details down."

"Oh yeah, of course. Well, yes, it was Josh. He likes to talk too much. I started imagining myself punching him in the face, except that's a terrible thing."

"Is it a terrible thing because you have powers? Or is it just a terrible thing in general? Would you still think it's terrible without the powers?" Catherine challenged. Liam laid back on the couch, thinking for a few seconds.

"I umm.. Yeah, bad in general. I still wouldn't want to punch anyone, even if I had no superpowers."

"So it was all just fantasizing and daydreaming? Something I'm sure everyone does as well. Just because you may once in a while fantasize about something doesn't mean you want to act on it," Catherine explained.

"I guess..." Liam reluctantly answered. He took a few seconds to think, but Catherine was quick to chime back in.

"How is your sexual life?" She shamelessly asked.

"Excuse me?" Liam responded, taken back.

"How is your sexual life? Although many may see it as taboo, it is part of life. Human beings, much like animals, have their urges and frustrations."

"It's nonexistent," Liam answered while blushing.

"When did it stop, when you got your superpowers? After you retired as a superhero? You're still a young man, after all."

"Once I got my superpowers," he admitted.

"Wow, that is a long time."

"I fear the result could be horrible."

"That is understandable. The unknown can always be scary, regardless of what it is. Sometimes we simply need to look for ways to slowly ease our way into things, slowly see what works and what doesn't without causing much damage," Catherine told him factually. Liam just sat there speechless as he stared at Catherine. This was turning out much different than what he had expected.

"I know, I know. You're probably thinking, what is this crazy lady asking me all these questions and getting so personal. My answer to you is the following: I am trying to make an assessment of you. I am trying to see how I will approach the issue and what may or may not work for you. Also, I apologize for failing to mention this: if you feel uncomfortable, you don't have to answer any questions," Catherine quickly summarized. Liam's heart began beating a little faster as he started to feel somewhat overwhelmed. It wasn't that he thought she was doing anything wrong; it was simply that he wasn't entirely used to this intensity.

Catherine must have noticed the overwhelmed look on his face because she smiled at him gently and leaned back against her chair. She wrote down a few things in her notebook before putting them aside and crossing her arms. She remained silent for a few moments, doing nothing but observing Liam, which also started to make him feel uncomfortable.

"I am sorry, I got a little too excited. Usually, I'm a bit more calm. Probably doesn't help that I've had four coffees throughout the day today," she admitted.

"It's alright, I understand. I'm just not used to it yet," Liam responded, trying not to sound offensive.
"Feel free to tell me to slow down and calm down. I don't take it personally. This is about you, not me, after all."

"Thank you," Liam added.

"Liam, what do you want to do differently for this week leading to our next session?"

"Better control of my emotions. Stay more positive," he replied truthfully.

"How will you do that?"

"I... I'm not sure...."

"Liam, how will you do that?" She asked him again. She saw his head tilt a bit and his eyes gazing at her. She could sense a form of resentment at that particular time.

"I know, I know. You are probably getting agitated and angry at me. I am here to help you. I want you to get better. For me to do that, I will be challenging you. As I mentioned before, all you have to do is tell me to slow down and stop. I could give you ideas on how you can go about changing your week. However, we are more likely to accomplish them if we come up with them ourselves," Catherine explained to him. She then stood up and smiled.

"Don't worry, I will give you some time to think. As a matter of fact..." She began saying as she approached a stand. She grabbed a sheet of paper and a pen. She handed them both to Liam and then hovered there, ready to explain.

"For the next ten minutes or so, I would like you to write down five things that went wrong last week. Then, I want you to write how they could have been avoided. It doesn't have to be fancy; even one-word responses could work. Afterward, I would like you to write two things you want to go right this week and how you will go about it. Don't stress it if you can't write anything down. The point of this exercise is to mainly get you thinking and challenging yourself," she told him and then took a second to catch her breath. She nodded at Liam and then pointed at the paper.

He noticed Catherine walk away from him and back to her stand, where she started flipping pages of one of her notebooks. He then looked back to his blank paper and started writing down the five things he felt went wrong with the week. That part was easy. Afterward, he began to struggle a bit with what to write. He thought that the answer to how he could have avoided them was as simple as controlling his emotions better, but then he felt like the answer was too simple. Was the explanation simply re-framing his thoughts? That sounded simplistic as well.

Liam glanced over Catherine's direction, noticing she was still reading through a notebook. Were those the notes that Stefanie had given her? They may have been notes that belonged to a different client. He finally decided not to think about it and wrote precisely what Stefanie would tell him, to re-frame his thoughts. After ten minutes on the mark, Catherine approached him and sat back on her chair.

"How did that go?" She casually asked him.

"I... I had a difficult time trying to figure out what to write. I felt like you may not like some of the answers," Liam admitted. Catherine smiled wide.

"Well, it wouldn't have mattered anyway. The exercise was more for you than for me. In fact, I will not even ask what you wrote down. I will simply tell you to keep that paper and look over it again once you return home."

"So all that... it was just for..." Liam started feeling a little puzzled.

"To get you to think. Get yourself to challenge your mind. It seems like you ended up doing that," she responded. Liam realized she wasn't wrong. She definitely was not like Stefanie, but he had been told so. He had been hesitant the entire session because of it, but perhaps it was time he embraced it, as Stefanie would have told him. He could imagine it in his mind, 'Different isn't bad. Different methods and approaches don't make any of them wrong.'

Rather than resisting, Liam decided to talk more freely for the remainder of the session. They mainly had a brief review of his two months with Stefanie and what had improved and what had not. She scheduled him for his next appointment at the same time the following week. He thanked her while leaving the room but never looked back as he left the building.

Chapter 20

When Liam opened his eyes that Monday morning, it felt like any other day. His days since seeing Catherine hadn't been terrible, aside from Josh's constant nasty remarks and bully-like laughter. Henry and Tati had been good in helping Liam divert his thoughts from Josh. He'd been to Henry's house several times and just sat there watching movies. Watching movies was something he hadn't done in a while. Still, they had all decided on comedies, so it had been better than he had anticipated. *'See, that wasn't so bad, was it? Once you do something, you sometimes find it that the idea of it was more terrifying than the actual thing,'* He imagined Stefanie telling him.

The other days, he had not gone over to Henry's house; he had made a trip to Mason's Bar. He had been reminded that Cole was away with his wife, but the bartenders there were friendly and easy to talk to. He did have a couple of nightmares and flashbacks, but overall, the days could have gone much worse. Which is why he had figured that Monday would be more or less the same.

The oddities started when he heard his cell phone ringing. It was unusual for him to receive any phone calls, never mind one at eight in the morning. He figured it would be spam and decided to let it ring through. Then, there was a notification noise; someone had left him a voicemail. *Odd,* he thought, since spam didn't generally leave any sort of voice messages. He quickly approached his phone and noticed the missed call was from his mother.

He had written a letter to her by hand not too long ago. While many people now would have simply chosen to write on the laptop and print it out or even just e-mail it, he liked the concept of writing it himself and sending it in the mail. He had told his mother a lot. After all, they hadn't seen or spoken to each other recently. He clicked on the voice message notification and listened to his mother's voice come on.

'Hey Liam, I am sorry I haven't gotten a chance to get back to you since I received your letter; your dad and I are going through some house renovations, so things have been a complete mess. I wanted to tell you I am so happy that you are doing better and that you took the step to start seeing a therapist. There is nothing wrong with that, and I have also done that. Give me a call back whenever you can. I would love to hear your voice,' she said before hanging up.

Liam stared at the phone a bit longer, deciding if he should call her now or if he should call her at a later time. A later time would be best. Despite his parents being morning people, he wasn't much of an early morning person. He put his phone back down firmly, deciding to call her after work or during his lunch break. It's not like he was much for phone talking anyhow.

He filled a glass of water in the kitchen and drank through it in seconds. After placing it down, he walked over to his refrigerator and opened it. It was empty, only a little in choice except for condiments. A shopping trip would also be in order soon. He decided that this would be the best time for him to do so. He only had work in the afternoon, and after work, he would find himself in either Henry's house or Mason's Bar, drinking either soda or Shirley Temple.

He dressed, went to his car, and drove to the closest grocery store. His experiences there had improved, though he had been ensuring to go at times when it was mainly empty. After filling his carriage, he walked to the cashier and paid for his items. As he headed towards his car, he felt like someone was watching him the entire time he was outside. He hadn't seen this person's face as they were wearing a long black coat with a hoodie underneath it. The hoodie covered the person's face.

Liam did not want to stare and make a deal out of it. It was probably nothing, just a man with a long black cloak. He'd seen many homeless people dressed like that. The fact he was staring at him was most likely just a coincidence, especially since Liam was the only person who had come out of the grocery store. Dismissing as anything else, he got into his car and drove back home.

Liam realized that Henry and Tati were off that day when he was putting his groceries away. Mason's Bar would be where he'd head to after work. He poured himself a bowl of cereal and sat on his couch. He ate everything inside the bowl, and then the waiting game came. Liam decided to head to work earlier to avoid seeing Josh at the entrance. Every day now, the prick would wait for him so he could make some snarky remark. Liam was still trying to figure out how the hostility had even started, but he guessed it didn't matter. Josh made his rounds, talking about everyone. Even Mike wasn't immune despite kissing Josh's ass constantly.

Liam found his usual parking spot and quickly left the car. He practically jogged inside the building. Soon, Josh and Mike would arrive and start smoking as they usually did. Liam went into the break room and waited there, a place he usually didn't spend much time inside. He counted the time until he could clock in and went to work quickly.

Surprisingly, Josh left him alone through the first half of his shift. Liam jumped into his car during his lunch break and took out his cell phone. He looked through the contacts list until he found his mother's number. It took three rings for her to answer.

"Liam? How are you doing?" She asked him.

"I'm doing good, Mom. It seems like everything might be getting better. I might put in for a vacation sometime and visit you and Dad," he told her.

"That would be great! Hopefully, the house renovations will be done, and you will be able to see how beautiful it looks," his mother added.

"I don't have much time right now; I'm on my lunch break," Liam told her.

"Oh yeah, of course, of course. Therapy is going well, then I take it?"

"It is. I had a new therapist this last week. She was different."

"Oh, so it's not that Stefanie anymore?"

"Only temporarily; she had a family emergency to attend to. She will be back. Catherine is different, but she is also effective in her own way," Liam explained.

"That's good then. The last thing you'd want is to end up with a terrible therapist and trust me, some do exist out there," she answered.

"Is Dad doing alright, too?" Liam managed to ask.

"Oh yes, he's doing good. He's just fairly stressed right now with all the renovations. The first contractor we hired completely messed something up, so he had to spend additional money and just hired new contractors," she explained to him.

"I'm sure the end result is going to look great. Dad always manages to stress out about things out of his control," Liam told her. As soon as he started saying the words, he realized how much it sounded like himself.

"Yeah, but he only takes it out on himself." The two then continued to catch up on the basic and simple things before he noticed that he had to return to work. He was going to be a few minutes late from his lunch. Despite that, he knew he would be fine; most people had done it at one point and never got in trouble.

"I'll talk to you soon again, Mom," he told her.

"I love you, Liam."

"I love you too, Mom," he answered, and they both hung up. He sighed and then left his car and returned to work.

Time passed, and it seemed as if everything was going to go smoothly; when there were only a couple of hours left of work, there were just two of them remaining in the room: Liam himself and Josh.

"I saw you. You came back from lunch late. Of course, Golden Boy gets told nothing from the boss," Josh mocked. Liam turned his face to Josh with an angry look.

"You're constantly late clocking in at the start of the shift, and he never tells you anything either. If anything, you're late more than I ever am."

"Oh yeah, the golden boy thinks he is better than me," Josh shouted. Liam nodded in disbelief.

"What have I done to you that gives you the urge to be a huge prick?" Liam demanded.

"You keep spending time with those weirdoes like you are better than me," Josh responded; he was walking around the warehouse, taking notes on a piece of paper. Liam started to feel more tense and frustrated. His face was slightly turning read, and his heart's beat hastened.

"Probably go around and talking shit about me; well, you can go and eat shit," Josh said, attempting to sound tough.

"Are you talking about me? You are constantly talking about everyone, including the man whose balls you always grab the moment you see, Mike," Liam scorned back. His anger levels were rising with every comment Josh made. He knew nothing good could come of this. He closed his eyes and decided to take a few deep breaths, trying to control himself and relax.

This isn't the time or place Liam, even if he does deserve it. This can't end well for both.

"Yeah, look at this fucking guy, do some work for once in your life," Josh remarked. Liam opened his eyes, turned around, and saw that Josh wasn't looking at him. Liam swung his fist, punching the leg of the steel in front of him. The leg bent immediately, and Liam quickly noticed that a heavy pallet resting at the top was now sliding down. Liam immediately panicked when he saw that it would fall on Josh. A pallet that heavy would either seriously injure Josh or, worse, kill him.

"MOVE!" Liam screamed. Luckily for him, Josh immediately realized and ran out of the way just as the pallet fell. There was a loud bang, and a huge mess was created. Liam looked around the ceiling in panic. There were no cameras that would have caught him punching the steel. Would Josh know, though?

"Holy fuck! This is what happens when a company buys cheap shit," Josh commented. It did not seem as if Josh suspected Liam. He would probably never imagine that a human could put a dent that big on a leg of steel. That, however, did not stop Liam's heart from pounding like it would blow up. His hands were shaking tremendously. He was frozen and in shock.

"You're not even going to fucking help me?" Josh screamed, pissed off. Liam nodded without saying a word and then grabbed the manager on duty.

Chapter 21

Liam was seated on the couch, his feet planted on the floor. His right foot was rapidly tapping without any signs of stopping. Catherine was just sitting, holding the notebook she had used the previous week. This time, she wore a skirt shorter than the one she wore the last week. She had certainly taken her time with makeup and her hair. She was also wearing high heels, and the scent of her perfume was quite mesmerizing.

"You don't look so well today," Catherine remarked while she prepared her pen.

"It wasn't a good end to my Monday," he replied, averting his eyes from her gaze.

"What happened on Monday?" Catherine asked.

"I... I almost... I almost killed someone," Liam divulged.

"Almost killed someone? Please elaborate," Catherine continued.

"At work. Josh. Well, he just can't... He just can't keep his mouth shut. So I just... I just kind of lost it and punched the leg of a steel in the warehouse. It dented it so badly that a pallet came sliding down and almost fell on top of him. It was heavy enough that it could have killed him," Liam confessed.

"I see. I take it you two were alone at that particular moment then?" Catherine asked.

"Yes... and he just wouldn't shut up...."

"Seems like he's been looking for trouble. How does he feel seeing you punch the steel like that?" She asked him while writing down a few notes.

"He didn't see. His back was turned. He thinks it was just cheap steel wearing down. There were no cameras to see it either."

"That's good then. Your identity is still intact."

"Yeah, but that's not the issue. The problem is that I allowed anger to get the best of me," Liam reiterated.

"It's not the first time, though, right? You've broken quite a few sinks," Catherine mentioned.

"Yeah, but it's always been inside my house. This was somewhere else, in public. I had never lost my cool like that in public, and lately, I feel like it's so easy for me to get angry."

"Liam, you need to sit back and take a few deep breaths. You are being too harsh on yourself. Things build up inside of us, and maybe one year ago, it wasn't as difficult to bottle up that anger, but the longer it keeps going, the harder it becomes to conceal. Despite the superpowers you may have, you are still a human with human emotions," Catherine explained to him.

"I... I..." Liam attempted to speak but was unable to.

"How was work the following day on Tuesday?"

"I called out. I didn't go. I think I may never go to work again; I might just quit, too," Liam said.

"Quit? Is that a wise decision?" Catherine asked him, a little surprised.

"Better than ending up hurting someone," Liam replied quickly.

"Have you thought about all other variables?"

"What variables?" Liam repeated, confused.

"You'll need money to pay for rent, food, any necessities. Also, your health insurance is through work, correct? You might not be able to make it to my or Stefanie's sessions anymore."

"What am I supposed to do? I can't risk doing something dumb like that ever again."

"Maybe you could always try to see if you and Josh can have different shifts. You can also try and take a week off of work; call it a traumatizing experience, watching a colleague almost being killed," Catherine suggested. Liam leaned back, still averting Catherine's gaze.

"I don't know... I don't know..."

"Well, do the week off to get some time to think. After a week, you can proceed if you still think quitting is the best choice. Right now, you're mainly in shock, which could lead to hasty decision-making."

"Take a leave from work, huh? Not long ago, I had taken a week off as well."

"Who cares? I can even write and sign a note relating to you being traumatized. They won't be able to do anything about it," she added. The idea of taking a week off was certainly enticing, but would it really change his mind about quitting altogether? This time, it was Josh; next time, it could end up being Mike or Chazz. What if Henry and Tati ever had a bad day, and somehow, he took it personally against them? There were so many things running through his mind.

"I guess taking the week off to think can't hurt," Liam conceded.

"Good! I'll write the note. You may need or not need it; in either case, you'll have it."

"Is that the only thing that came from this week?"

"I also got to speak to my mom for a bit; I'm thinking I might end up visiting her soon," Liam added.

"That's good. The sense of familiarity could be very helpful. Did you speak to your mom before or after the incident?"

"It was before, coincidentally on the same day."

"Anything you two spoke about that could have increased your rage for later?"

"No, not at all," he responded quickly.

"That's good. Sometimes the catalyst for something could originate somewhere else entirely," she explained.

Liam remained still, debating whether Josh himself had been his own catalyst or if something else was slowly growing inside him. Even before Stefanie left, he felt his emotions were going up and down, much like a roller coaster. Catherine must have noticed that he was thinking about it, too, because she decided to speak.

"What is on your mind?" She asked him carefully.

"Just trying to pinpoint and see if something is going wrong with me in general," Liam admitted.

"You're just stressing yourself more. You are a human being like the rest of us. We all get angry sometimes. We all go through downward moods and upward moods. It is all part of life," Catherine told him. Liam attempted to take his mind elsewhere, but it wasn't as simple as it seemed.

"When I was younger and in college, there were days when I felt like I was the greatest thing in the world. There were other days when I felt like I was the worst thing in the world. And then there were days when I felt horrible because I felt like I was the greatest thing in the world. Perhaps that last part may not make much sense, but it is the reality of it," Catherine told him.

"If I had no powers, at least I would have much less to worry," Liam blurred out.

"Well, I think just about anyone will say something similar. They'll simply replace powers with something else that they feel is a curse in their lives. Maybe if I didn't have this job, maybe if I didn't have this partner, maybe if I had different parents, maybe if I had more money, and so on and on. No matter where you look or go, excuses will always exist and be there. There is nothing wrong with us for it. It is just in our nature."

"If it's natural, in our nature, then how do we live with it?" Liam asked, hoping for one straight answer.

"Liam, there really isn't a right answer for that. It's different for everyone; it comes down to acceptance and how you get there; it is up to you."

"Acceptance? Acceptance of what?"

"Accepting that there are things outside of your control. Accepting that what's done is done. Accepting that you can still live. Accepting that you will still make mistakes. Accepting just about anything," Catherine added.

"So ultimately, I just need to figure out how I can get myself to accept that I have these powers and will have to go through the rest of my life with them?" Liam asked.

"I don't know, Liam, you tell me," she casually responded.

Chapter 22

Liam sat by the rocks while enjoying the occasional splash of water as the waves came crashing against them. Quite a few people were there for an afternoon during the week. Most people there were mothers or fathers with their kids or elderly people. The sun was shining down on his face at that point. He was thankful for the warmer weather. The cold wasn't exactly his thing.

Earlier in the morning, he had called his boss, asking for him to take a week off. He had used the excuse of feeling distraught by the sight of a colleague almost being crushed. To his surprise, he had not been met with much resistance. 'Of course, of course. Josh himself is taking a month off from the trauma. We're also going to be closed for a couple of days as they need to look into the safety of the building. Liam, if you need a second week, just let me know. I will approve it,' his boss had told him. Perhaps they were afraid of getting sued, and in a way, Liam felt terrible. He knew nothing was defective about the steel or any of the equipment. It had been him and him alone.

Part of him wished there had been a camera; at least he would have been caught rather than being a coward and keeping it quiet. He continued to sit there, watching the water and the boats in the distance, enjoying the nice weather. To his right was a small beach where a dog enjoyed himself chasing after a tennis ball. If only life was that simple. After sitting there for roughly a few hours, he decided it was time to return home.

He drove for about twenty minutes before finally reaching his street. As he parked his car, he saw someone a couple of blocks away wearing a long black jacket. It was relatively too warm to be wearing a coat. Yet something felt familiar for some odd reason. He couldn't see the person's face; it was hidden by a hoodie underneath the jacket. He'd seen this person before when he had gone shopping. Was this person following him? Did they know him? The most important question he had was, was the person real? No way someone would wear a hoodie and a jacket on a t-shirt type of weather.

He closed the door of his car and began walking steadily. Taking casual steps so as not to spook this person. Just as he got closer to the stranger, the person turned around and began running away. Annoyed, Liam swung his fist into the air but decided he wouldn't chase anyone. At least now he knew that whoever this person was was definitely following him. That or they did not exist, and he was getting even crazier than before.

He walked up the steps to his door and quickly unlocked it. Once inside, he checked his cell phone for the first time. As he expected, there were no new notifications. What was he expecting? Not like he had any friends or knew anyone. He had already spoken with Henry and Tati right after what had happened, so they were updated. He glanced over at the couch again and then rolled his eyes. The journal was still there and untouched. He bought it right after his first session with Stefanie and has neglected it ever since. He just never felt motivated enough to actually write on it. Perhaps there was a fear of letting out his true feelings.

He walked over to his bedroom and stood in front of a wall. On the wall hung the painting that Stefanie had lent him right before leaving. He couldn't help but smile a bit as he looked at it. It was no longer the actual message or meaning of the painting that came to mind. It was his session with Stefanie. It wasn't that he disliked Catherine; she was very good herself. She was different, though. That was the best way he could describe it, different. He had felt more at peace with himself in his sessions with Stefanie. The truth was, it was probably a comfort factor. He had grown comfortable with Stefanie, so now his mind was resisting the new therapist. It certainly wasn't fair to Catherine.

He opened the windows in his room before lying in bed with his stomach facing up. Quick flashes of dust and smoke around him started running through his mind. *Not now... Leave me in peace.* It was soon followed by voices, *'You killed my mommy,'* followed by an older voice, *'How can you live with yourself?'* He closed his eyes for a second and very quickly started filling his mind with thoughts of what could have been a different life. He stood before a lovely house, opening the door and enjoying a fresh smell while walking inside. He heads to his backyard and lights a candle on a table. He sits on the chair and lays back in what feels like the most relaxing feeling ever.

Once he opened his eyes back up, an additional half-hour had passed. The remainder of his day was uneventful, but he would get to do it all over again the following day. Henry and Tati had both texted him to see if he wanted to hang out. He declined the offer, wanting to stay away from people for a little while, at least until he could figure himself out.

He attempted to waste as much time as possible throughout the day. He cooked while slow music played on his Bluetooth speaker. He even attempted to pick up a book and read it, but after reading two words, he put it away. His mind just wasn't motivated enough to read. He bathed in hot water as usual, lay on his bed some more, paced around his house, and decided to check the internet.

His journey through the internet lasted only a short time. With every place he went to scroll around, he found nothing but a wave of negativity. He decided to leave before he'd start to truly get angry. He took a few deep breaths and then jumped into the bed. It wasn't without struggle, but the day passed, and somehow, he fell asleep.

Another day arrived, and he was up early as usual. He did his usual morning routine and headed to the beach again as he had done the previous morning. He left the house and was relieved to see it was just as warm as the previous day. He looked across the street and saw Josh standing there, giving him the dirtiest look, even for Josh himself. Josh raised his hand and flipped Liam off. Confused, Liam looked both ways before he crossed the street, and then, just like that, Josh vanished. Liam quickly closed his eyes and shook his head a few times. Once he opened his eyes, it seemed clear he had imagined Josh. As he was about to cross the street again to head towards his car, he noticed the exact figure with a long black jacket down the block.

"Hey, you!" Liam shouted as he began walking rapidly towards the stranger. The stranger turned around quickly and started to jog away from Liam. *Not this time fucker.* Liam thinks as he starts running after the stranger. He knew he could easily catch up by flying or dashing, but he didn't want to bring that kind of attention to himself. He ran faster than the stranger, which allowed him to catch up. The moment he attempted to grab the stranger by the shoulders, they were no longer there.

"Huh?" Liam spoke up. He was confused; was the figure really just in his mind? There was no other explanation. He was starting to lose it; it had to be. He then turned around and saw the stranger standing by his car.

"Too slow," the stranger shouted out in a muffled voice. Liam began to feel himself get angry. He turned around and started running towards the car as fast as possible.

"Can't do shit about it, you're a killer. Live with it," the same muffled voice yelled out to him. Liam didn't stop until he reached his car and swung his fist toward the stranger, who vanished again. Liam's hand went through the window, shattering the glass all over his driver's seat. He removed his hand and stared at it in disbelief, his fist still closed. He had once again allowed himself to lose control of his temper. He continued looking at his fist in disbelief. There was no way the figure was real. His mind was starting to hallucinate. The problem was worsening, something he would have to mention to Catherine in their next session. Should he even attend? This was a reason to attend.

The beach was out of the question. He would have to take the time to clean all the glass shards from inside his car and then tape up his window until he'd have the opportunity to replace it. He spent a good hour alone just cleaning up all the glass. Then it took him another good forty minutes just getting packing tape on his window. Once he was done, he decided to head back inside his house. He was done with the day. He needed to stay away from potentially causing any more trouble.

Back inside his house, he attempted to keep his mind at bay. It wasn't working out well. He sat on his couch with his foot tapping rapidly as he kept recalling the moment he punched the car window. If he was hallucinating Josh showing up across the street and some stranger stalking him. What else could he be hallucinating? How could he differentiate what was real and what wasn't? He wanted answers and straightforward answers, not answers without actual answers. Why couldn't anyone just tell him how to think, feel, and live without always telling him it was on him to figure out those answers.

You're losing it, man.

Shut up.

Don't start making excuses for your lack of control. No one can help you if you can't even take the steps to help yourself.

Shut up.

You decided to try to be the hero and follow a villain around, which resulted in you getting the powers. It is your fault for not allowing the professionals to handle it.

I know. Shut up.

Were you expecting to get some sort of medal for finding their little hideout?

People were getting killed and taunted by that man. Shut up.

And you made the world so much better with all those people killed and property damaged.

People could have lost a lot more if no one existed to stop those supervillains. Now shut up.

Is that what you tell yourself nowadays to sleep at night?

Shut up.

Liam's foot never once stopped tapping. His mind was racing uncontrollably. Tears started coming down his eyes. It wasn't long ago that he thought he was getting better, controlling his emotions easier. It was all an illusion, a simple lie he had told himself to keep going. He stood up from his couch and screamed while waving his hands in the air, tears running down his face. Veins popped up angrily from his neck. He ran to his room and sat in a corner, his knees up and his arms wrapped around them.

After time had passed, and he felt himself calm down a little more, he stood up and opened the closet door. Inside, lying on the floor, was a good-sized safe. He reached for the combination wheel but froze when he was inches from touching it. He moved his hands away and closed the closet door.

"No," he said softly.

Chapter 23

Liam slowly walks down the hallway when he notices the door to Catherine's office open. Leaving is a client for which he can't quite make out the face. The person is wearing a gray hoodie with the word Dreams written in big letters on the front. The day was fairly chillier than the entire week, and Liam regretted coming in with a t-shirt. As they walked past each other, Liam still could not look into the person's face; they were just staring at the ground while walking. They must have been someone shy and awkward around others.

Liam then noticed Catherine standing outside her door with a big smile, waving for him to head over. Once he reached her office, he entered with a slight bow and headed toward his usual spot on the couch. He sat there and waited for Catherine to close the door and take her seat after grabbing her notebook. She flipped through a few pages slowly and crossed her legs as she got comfortable. She had excellent posture, he thought.

"So, are you excited?" She quickly asked him.

"Excited?" He answered, a little confused by the question.

"Stefanie is due back in a couple of weeks or so. You may only have two or three more sessions left with me. You're probably thinking, oh, thank goodness I don't have to see this crazy lady again after," she joked.

"Of course not. I think you've been very good," Liam told her. Catherine's smile widened.

"Don't worry, I won't take offense of you wanting to return to her. You were and are still her client, after all," Catherine noted.

"It just became a comfort level thing."

"Oh, no worries, Liam. I've had the pleasure of meeting you and having you here. Though we still have at least two more sessions anyways," she added.

"Yeah, of course, it's been nice meeting you as well," Liam answered.

"Tell me about your week, Liam. You don't seem quite excited even with the news of Stefanie returning."

"It's been a rough week, if I'm being honest. Did you get updates on her mother and the surgery? I've been meaning to ask, but it always evades my mind."

"Her mother is doing fine. Everything went smoothly. How come it was a rough week?"

"I think I'm hallucinating," he admitted.

"Hallucinating? Oh boy, that could be frustrating. What exactly are you hallucinating?" She asked him.

"Well... At one point, I thought I saw Josh across the street from my house flipping me off."

"Wow, you even hallucinated him flipping you off. Seems like at least you keep the personalities intact," Catherine added jokingly. She had hoped to lighten the mood up but with no success. After noticing the look on Liam's face, her smile faded, and she got into her professional demeanor again.

"What else did you hallucinate?" She asked him.

"I keep seeing this person with a long black jacket and a hoodie underneath it. I can never see this person's face, but every time I get close to them, the person vanishes. I am starting to think that if I see what is underneath the hoodie, it'll be my face. The things it shouts at me are so similar that my own mind sometimes tells me," he explained to her. She was attentively listening and intrigued by it. The tropical smell in the room was quite strong, perhaps even more potent than in the previous sessions.

"Hmm. Anything in particular that could be causing the hallucinations? Have you found any way to stop them?" She asked him.

"They seem to only happen when I'm outside. I also ended up punching the window of my car, once again allowing anger to take over me."

"Interesting. Seems like this is the second time in the last month that anger has gotten the best of you," Catherine pointed out. Liam looked at her facial expression as she raised an eyebrow at him. "What are you thinking?" He asked her.

"Maybe that could be the next thing we focus on, diminishing those anger outbursts."

"Like anger management?" He asked, puzzled.

"Well, something like that," she answered truthfully.

"I mean, I used to have these episodes, but they were always inside my house. The sink used to be the only victim of those outbursts. Now I started getting closer to people, and it seems to be getting out of control more."

"Interesting. Perhaps getting closer to people wasn't the right approach, huh?" Catherine mentioned.

"I don't know... It seemed like a good idea... Stefanie had challenged me to... I mean, I was at work for over a year... Nothing had ever happened...."

"Stefanie is an amazing human being. She always means well. She also never sees a glass half empty or half full. She says that if that water went into a smaller glass, that glass would be full," Catherine explained.

"I don't quite understand."

"Understand what Liam?"

"Understand what you're trying to tell me."

"That maybe, for this particular case, Stefanie's advice could have been off. Look, Liam, we are therapists; we go to school for it, but we are also human beings. That means we aren't always one hundred percent right. It's not that she did anything wrong, not that you did anything wrong, but you are a special case, Liam. You have gone through things like no one else has gone through. Perhaps the genetic advice and methods aren't exactly built for you. Perhaps we need to get more creative and try new approaches," Catherine explained to him. Liam was speechless. He didn't know how to respond or what to believe in.

"I'm sorry, Liam. You probably think I'm being a bitch, but I assure you I am not trying to be one. I am just trying to be honest so we can figure out what is happening and help you. You are still young. Shit, you're younger than I am; there are still so many years ahead of you. I don't want you to keep going feeling distraught like this. That could be a harrowing life. I don't know how I'd do it if I lived my life feeling tormented daily."

"I... I... I'm... I'm not sure what to say," Liam admitted.

"You don't have to say anything, Liam. We'll just continue our sessions and figure it out. Once Stefanie returns, I'll hand her some of my notes and see what she thinks and feels about them," Catherine told him. For whatever reason, Liam felt uncomfortable, confused, and completely lost. He no longer knew what to think. Catherine had made some good points. Was he wrong to want to go back to Stefanie? Was he more interested in returning to Stefanie because she let him have his way more? Perhaps he needed someone more like Catherine, who would call out things as they were rather than try to turn everything into a rainbow.

"Tell me, Liam. Did anything else weird happen to you during the week?" Catherine asked him.

"There was another day during the week that I went for a walk around the town. During the walk, I kept seeing this figure wearing a black jacket. They were hiding behind something every time I looked in their direction. At that point, I figured I was already hallucinating things, so I decided to simply ignore it. However, during my walk, I kept hearing people shouting at me. I couldn't differentiate if it was my imagination or if it really was happening. I was feeling so lost and angry at that point. Part of me wanted to cry. Another part of me wanted to unleash that anger."

"What sort of things were these people shouting?"

"They were shouting things like looser, wus, and even the famous go fuck yourself," Liam told her.

"Interesting, and you couldn't tell if it was real or imagination?" Catherine asked him, intrigued.

"Well... I kind of knew it was my imagination, but it felt so real."

"Interesting. Anything else?"

"It's about it. I'm sure I'll have more to discuss next week," Liam responded.

"Alright, let's try a little exercise. Let's go back to a few years when you decided to stop being a superhero. What happened in your battle against the last supervillain you would ever face? Right before destroying a few illegal scientific laboratories? As far as I remember, they never did find the body of that last supervillain," Catherine pointed out. Liam started scratching his hair uncontrollably. There was a moment when he was about to say something. He then stopped himself and rethought his answer for a moment.

"I'm sorry, but what does that have to do with this?" He respectfully asked.

"Could try to pinpoint the origins of that anger or the voices in your head. Did you hear them before that battle?"

"Sort of. I used to yeah, but they weren't as powerful. They became more and more powerful with time," Liam added.

"How come the last villain you fought was the one they never found?" Catherine asked. Liam glanced over the ceiling and then back to Catherine.

"I don't want to talk about it. I want to move forward. I need to go home. Put me down for the same time next week," Liam told her respectfully while standing up.

"I'm sorry, Liam. I didn't mean to upset you. I'm just trying to help you."

"I know. But I... I just need to go home right now. I'll be back next week, I promise," he assured her while heading towards the door. Catherine didn't make any more attempts to stop him. She watched him leave the room without looking back or saying another word.

Chapter 24

It was a scorching day as the sun shone bright up above. Liam stood in front of an old-looking building. It resembled the building where he'd received his powers five years prior. This is what the criminal scientists had done: purchased a few buildings around the country and rotated through them to try and avoid being caught. They had been able to hide for a while, but not anymore. Liam had been tipped; this was his last duty before entirely giving up his Faceless persona. To destroy all the buildings that were still creating any sort of superhumans. He held up the bomb he had in his hand and began walking towards the building.

* * *

When Liam returned to his senses, he sat on a little park bench. He had destroyed a total of five labs within the same day. It was his way to ensure it all came to a stop. It had worked; no supervillain had been seen in two years. He began to see quick flashes of a body lying on the debris of a destroyed building. The face was covered by another rock, but Liam could hear his words as clearly as he had two years prior. 'How can you live with yourself?' Those had been the last words of the last supervillain he had ever faced.

He looked up and saw the same figure he had been seeing for the last week across the street. He rolled his eyes, unable to figure out what was triggering his hallucinations. Liam cautiously turned his eyes towards a kid who was now standing right in front of him. The kid stayed quiet for a few seconds, then raised his hand and pointed at Liam.

"Are you going to kill my mommy too?" The kid calmly asked him.

"Huh? What?" Liam responded flustered.

"Don't cry, I'll just be an orphan," the kid replied. Liam started shaking his head. Was this kid another part of his imagination? It certainly didn't feel like it, as the kid's mother quickly grabbed her child and walked away from Liam with a dirty look. Maybe the kid hadn't been the illusion, just the words spoken. Everything was becoming confusing. It was becoming increasingly difficult to tell what was real and what wasn't. He had decided to ask for another week at work to try and figure things out. It had been quickly approved.

Henry and Tati had been trying to contact him, but he had not responded to their texts or calls. It was better off for them. The way everything had been going, he would only end up hurting them. They were good people. They did not deserve to be put at risk. He sighed as he stood up and then walked over to his car. His driver's side window was smashed, shards of glass all over the driver's seat. The same window that he had punched through not long ago, either. Did he do it again and not remember it? Everything was quickly becoming more and more frustrating at that point. He wanted to cry, fall to his knees, and let it all out, but not there. He felt that too many people would look at him and think of him as an idiot. He cleared up as much of the shards from the seat as possible before getting inside his car, turning on the engine, and pulling out of the parking space.

At first, he managed to keep his face expressionless, but slowly, his eyes became more watery, and in no time, tears were sliding down his face. He managed to find somewhere secluded and parked. He put his head against the steering wheel and began to cry without holding back.

Why did it feel like things were getting so much worse for him? Why was he not able to gather control of his life? Stefanie would be back soon; she'd be able to talk him up. Would she, though? Catherine was trying, but somehow, it had a different effect than Stefanie. Then again, he wasn't even sure if Stefanie would be able to help him out either. Maybe it wasn't because it was someone different. Maybe there was no salvation for him at all. He was the problem, not Catherine or Stefanie.

He felt some of the breeze coming from his window as he cried. Every day, he felt more and more distanced from himself. He didn't even know how that was possible. His life had taken a turn; he no longer felt like going to Mason's Bar, and he no longer felt like seeing Tati and Henry. He just wanted... He didn't know what he wanted. He pulled his head back up, breathing heavily. He felt like punching the steering wheel but managed to hold back.

He took out his phone, found his mother on his contact list, and called her number. He didn't know who else to call. He wasn't even sure what he was going to talk about. However, this was not a moment he wanted to be left with his own thoughts. It wouldn't matter what the conversation would end up being. He couldn't take it or handle his own mind at that moment. The phone rang twice before his mother answered.

"Liam? How are you doing?" She calmly asked.

"I don't know mom... I don't know..." He said as he attempted to hold back more tears. Ever since he had gained his superpowers, he hadn't been as close to his family as he would have liked. He knew it was all his fault. He had purposely created distance and kept himself away from them. Had it been the right choice? He believed so. It had kept them safe from himself.

"Honey, you don't sound too well. What is going on?" She asked, concerned.

"Just a bad day, Mom. That's all. Just a bad day. Someone broke the window of my car, so I'm just overreacting, that is all," he answered.

"The window of your car? Why? Did they steal anything? Are you ok?" She quickly asked him.

"I'm fine, I'm fine. They took nothing. There was nothing to take anyway. I want you to know I love you and am sorry."

"I love you too, but why are you sorry?" His mother asked, sounding even more concerned.

"I haven't been a perfect son in the last seven years. I let you all down."

"You couldn't let me down if you tried, Liam. You grew up. You became your own person, life happens. I know young years can be such a struggle," his mother answered.

"I could have been better," Liam reiterated.

"Liam, please don't do anything foolish. You have not disappointed anyone. You have always been strong and resilient; whatever you are dealing with, you will defeat it."

"I hope so," he barely managed to say as more tears started crawling down his face. He put his free hand over his face and then took a deep breath before speaking again.

"I got to go, Mom. I'll call you soon, ok? I'll be ok," he told her, still unsure whether he believed it.

"Alright, I love you, Liam. Call me any time you need to," she told him.

"I will," he answered and hung up the phone. He threw it to the passenger's seat and started to drive home. A couple of neighbors sat on a chair on a sidewalk, enjoying the warm weather. One of them noticed the window broken on Liam's car and pointed to it just as Liam stepped out.

"What happened?" The elderly man asked while he relaxed in his chair with an iced coffee in his right hand.

"I uh... I accidentally threw a baseball there."

"Sheesh, expensive mistake," the elderly man responded. Liam faked a smile and nodded.

"Yeah, silly me." He then walked over to his door and entered the house quickly. He ran to his room and lay down, with his stomach facing down, and immediately put his head between his pillows. He started to feel his cell phone vibrating inside the pockets of his jeans, but he ignored it. He was not currently in the mood or the mindset to talk to anyone. He lay there as still as possible, in a void of nothing but inner pain. After his tears had faded, so did his consciousness.

By the time he woke up, it was roughly two thirty in the morning. It was the most sleep he'd gotten in quite a while. Yet he still felt like he hadn't slept in days. He rolled his eyes. He did not feel like getting up, but he needed to use the restroom. For a moment, he couldn't remember why he was so depressed, and then, all at once, the memories seeped in again.

His thoughts then shifted to something else: his job. He had been able to get another week off of work, yet he had to decide to either stay or quit his job permanently. At the time, he was leaning toward quitting his job. Perhaps he could find work from his house or, at the very least, away from people. The one thing that left him uncertain was if he could not find another job, how would he pay all of his bills? Would he be able to continue seeing Stefanie without his health insurance? It was a difficult choice, and he didn't know what to do or think about it. Life would be so much easier if it had an actual manual telling him how to handle each situation. Instead, he had to lie in his bed and stress about it.

Every day that passed, Liam simply stayed inside his house. He felt that it was the best decision that he could make. For whatever reason, when he was inside his home, he didn't hallucinate. He still had to deal with his flashbacks and sounds of the past, but at least no hallucinations to add to the problem.

Henry and Tati had been trying to reach him throughout the week, but he had simply ignored them and spent most of his days in the bathtub, in bed, or in the toilet. It had become quite the routine when Wednesday finally came around. It was therapy session day. This could even be his last session with Catherine. Stefanie was due back soon, and the thought of it brought him some excitement.

Like all the other times he had gone to Catherine, he took a few minutes to look at the painting he'd taken from Stefanie's office. It was the only time lately he actually managed a genuine smile, despite being a small and weak one. He left the house and was reminded of something he'd already forgotten when he arrived at his car. His driver's window was still broken, and he hadn't even taped it up like last time. Eventually, he would get to it, but now it was time to drive to his appointment.

Chapter 25

Liam strolled towards Catherine's door. Unlike the previous times, no one appeared to be leaving her office. Her previous appointment must have ended early. He closed his hand into a fist and gently knocked on the door several times. Rather than having the door open for him as he usually did, he heard a voice from the other side.

"Come in," Catherine's voice told him. It was odd; her tone didn't appear to have any emotion or life. Perhaps it was just him overthinking things once again. He reached for the handle and turned the knob. As he slowly opened the door, he noticed that Catherine was already sitting on her chair. Her left hand held her head while her shoulder rested on the chair's armrest. Liam squinted, confused and wary, as he felt that the energy in the room wasn't what it usually was. He gently closed the door, walked to the couch, and sat. At first, he couldn't see her face, but he felt something was off.

"How was your week?" She asked with a very monotone voice.

"It wasn't good at all," he responded, still trying to decipher what was happening.

"I'm sorry to hear that," she answered with the same tone. She was still not looking at him. Instead, she was looking toward the wall. She did not have a notebook to take notes or anything. Liam wanted to look at her face, but he felt any attempt would be rude. He laid back on the couch, waiting for Catherine to speak, but she remained quiet longer.

Silence filled the room, making it easy for Liam to feel uncomfortable. No one spoke; it sounded like Catherine may have been sobbing. Had she gotten in trouble for something? Perhaps something had happened in her family, which was not a good day for her. Liam rubbed his mouth for a few seconds and then opened his mouth a few times, trying to speak but stopping himself every time.

"I still keep hallucinating," Liam mentioned, wondering if it would even make a difference.

"That's certainly not good," Catherine slowly replied. Liam leaned back on the couch, once again feeling uncomfortable. He looked around. There were still no changes to the wall; the room had the same tropical smell as always, and he was still as pathetic as ever.

"Stefanie returns next week, right?" He casually asked her. She was silent momentarily before finally spilling, "Oh," a statement that confused Liam.

"Oh? What does that mean?" He casually asked. His heart's beat slowly increased with every second of silence. Catherine remained quiet, not even looking in his direction.

"I'm sorry, but... What is going on? You seem very different today, and the whole Oh, with Stefanie?" Liam demanded. She slowly started to look in his direction, and he could see the redness in her eyes, like someone who had crying for a while already. Tears of sorrow and sadness.

"What happened?" Liam asked, standing up. His lungs felt like they were getting crushed like he had to start grasping for air.

"It's... It's... It's about Stefanie," she managed to slowly add. Liam's mouth opened wide in shock and took several steps forward. There was incredible pain in his chest, his heart? Most likely not. A panic attack was more likely. He started taking quick breaths and continued to do his best to restrain his emotions.

"She was driving a car. She was driving back to her mother's house at night, and then..."

"And then what?" Liam demanded, sounding a little more aggressive than he had wanted.

"There was a drunk driver..."

"What did the drunk driver do?" Liam asked, a little angry.

"Liam, please calm down. I can see you are getting angry and emotional, and I understand that. But please, don't do anything foolish."

"Anything foolish? You still haven't told me what happened!" Liam screamed loudly.

"The driver caused an accident... Stefanie didn't make it," Catherine finally told him.

Liam froze immediately. It was like he was no longer in the same world. It felt like he was floating in the vacuum of space for the rest of eternity. This was not what he wanted or needed to hear. He became lost in his thoughts, and his entire world caught fire around him and then collapsed. He couldn't breathe, and his heart skipped a beat. He quickly turned to look at the door and began to walk towards it, and then Catherine stood up.

"Liam. I know it is difficult right now. I know your emotions are probably running wild, but I don't think you should be alone right now."

"Yeah, why is that?" He coldly asked her.

"You may end up doing something you could regret."

"I have done so many things that I regret," he casually told her.

"Perhaps, but isn't that why you come here? To try and not do any more of those things? To try and suppress those nightmares and voices?"

"Stefanie was a good person, and now she's gone..." He barely managed to say.

"Alongside many other good people every single day. It sucks, it really does, Liam, but this is the world that we are living in," Catherine explained to him.

"I don't know, I just... I don't know..." Liam responded as he collapsed to his knees in tears. He could still envision Stefanie's smile in his mind. He could still see her adjusting her glasses while speaking to him in her usual calm and peaceful tone. Now, he would never get to experience that ever again. No one would. Someone had made a choice to drive while drunk, and in return, it had ended someone else's life. A great person's life.

"Liam, I'm going to step outside for a little bit to get some fresh air. Stay here, and take a few minutes to breathe," Catherine told him. She gently put her hand on his shoulder and then left the room. There was quietness again. Liam attempted to realign his mind again, but it wasn't working. He was frozen on his knees and completely zoned out.

The flashbacks from his past as Faceless were more potent than ever. This time, it was the faces of the bodies lying on the ground; this is how every one of these people's families had felt. No. They must have felt much worse; they were family-related through DNA. What had he done? Everyone always dreamed of being a superhero and all the great things they could do. No one ever thinks about what the consequences can be. Like someone driving under the influence, nothing could ever go wrong with them. 'I drive my best when drunk,' 'Don't worry, I'm a great drunk driver,' was what everyone would always tell themselves. Now here he was, hating on the driver that took Stefanie's life, so angry that he could go and give this man a piece of his fist. And yet he himself was a driver that took many lives.

Liam stood back up and rushed to the door. As he opened the door, Catherine was on her way inside. They exchanged looks for a few seconds before Catherine shook her head gently in disapproval.

"I need to go. Don't worry about me," he told her and then walked away. He found himself getting into his car as quickly as he possibly could. He drove pretty recklessly but was able to make it back home without being pulled over.

The first thing he did when he made it home was head into his bedroom and open the closet door. He stared at the safe for a few seconds, giving it quite a dirty look. He reached for it and unlocked it. Inside was his former Faceless costume alongside his mask. He grabbed the plain silver mask and looked into it. He could see his reflection on it, and it disgusted him to no end. It was time for him to get rid of it all. He placed them back in the safe and locked it up again. He knew exactly where and how he would be getting rid of it. Though he would have to wait for the middle of the night to do it.

Chapter 26

The middle of the night had arrived. It was roughly two thirty in the morning, and very few would be awake. He opened the window in his room and then looked around and noticed no lights on, and no one was present. It helped that there was little visibility in his bedroom to begin with. He put on a black hoodie and then covered his face with it. He then easily picked up the safe from his closet and flew out the window. He went as high as he felt he should so he wouldn't be spotted. While holding the safe with both hands, he started to fly fast, away from his house and town. It was time to get rid of his so-called superhero costume.

He flew and flew until he finally made it to the beach. He paused for a second, looked around, and continued to fly deeper into the ocean until he could no longer see the sand or buildings. This was perfect; it would never be found here. He dropped the safe into the water and watched it sink. His heart still ached with the loss of Stefanie, but watching the safe disappear and sink deep below the sea gave him a sense of potential for a new beginning. Something would still need to be done about the powers, something he still needed to figure out how to approach.

He sighed, flipped off the spot where he had dropped the safe, and then flew back towards the beach. The smell and sound of the sea actually felt nice this time. It soothed him, even if just for a few seconds. Once back at the beach, he descended to the sand instead of flying home. It was empty, and no one was around. Once again, it was simply the sounds of the waves as they crashed onto the sand. No hallucinations were happening, either. Probably because his mind was already heavy for the day.

He had spent a good hour at the beach when he decided it was best for him to fly back home. Any later might start risking him being sighted by a very early riser. Like before, he flew high enough that anyone would unlikely notice him. His flight home went reasonably smoothly, and he entered his home the same way he had exited, through his bedroom window. Once inside, he closed it and walked on over to the painting that Stefanie had given him. He took the painting down and placed it on his bed.

He walked over to the living room and approached the couch. He

Andre Pereira

picked up the journal for the first time since he had bought it and walked back to his bedroom. He got a hold of a pen and sat back on his bed. This was rather painful for him, but he felt he owed it to Stefanie to write in the journal. Slowly, he raised his hand; it trembled with grief. He moved the tip of the pen to the paper and slowly moved it, forming the words on the page. Tears filled his eyes as he couldn't stop thinking about what she must have been going through while it was happening. What all those people he had hurt were going through during his battles.

The law had never really made any attempts to go after Faceless. After all, they knew he'd been their only way of stopping all these other supervillains, so why would they want to stop him? Faceless had never really been involved with petty crimes and small-time criminals. His focus had been the super-powered people, and because of that, he had never fallen into a wanted list. Yet, Liam felt as if he should have. He continued to write for the remainder of the night, and despite him being due back at work, he was confident he would be calling out.

* * *

Time had passed, and after having written everything he had wanted to, he had managed to close his eyes and get a little bit of sleep. As anticipated, he called out of work, realizing he was probably never returning. The moment that stores began to open up, he went out shopping. He bought a couple of shipping boxes and more oversized envelopes. Once he returned home, he packed the painting into a box, placed the journal in an envelope, and added it inside the box. He stood in front of his bed momentarily, staring at the box. His eyes were red and watery. Grief was still filling him on the inside.

After a good ten minutes of just standing, he finally picked up the box and left his house. He opened his car door, remembering his driver's seat window was still missing. There was no telling when he would get that fixed now. He didn't have any motivation, any will for anything. It was as if he was becoming a robot. He was a person without emotions. He started his car and drove towards the post office, where he dropped the box off, paid for the shipping, and left.

He made his way back home right after and took a seat on the couch. For the first time in what must have been three months, there was no journal on the sofa. He didn't put any music on, and he didn't turn on the television either. He just sat there without emotions or thought and in complete silence. He jumped a little when his cell phone started to vibrate. He lifted the phone with his right hand and looked to see who was calling him. It was Catherine. Puzzled, he clicked the green button on the screen and put the phone next to his ear.

"Liam, are you there?" Catherine asked. *Of course I'm here, who the hell do you think answered the phone?* He thought with frustration.

"Yes," he managed to respond.

"Good. Good. I've been worried about you, Liam. I know you really liked Stefanie. I know you were looking forward to going back to her, and I don't take that personally at all. Stefanie was a great friend of mine, too. It's also been tough for me," she explained to him. How could he have been so selfish? Of course, she was going through it as well. She knew Stefanie longer and better than he ever did. Yet he was acting like he had been the only one affected.

"I'm sorry. I just... I don't deal with grief quite well," he admitted.

"That's ok, Liam. Everyone handles it differently. That's just how emotions operate. Anyways, there is another reason why I called you," Catherine pointed out.

"What is it?" Liam asked, sounding a bit cold.

"As I've mentioned, I know you adored Stefanie, and she was a very good friend of mine. Maybe we could grab dinner together and reminisce on her. Nothing creepy or unprofessional, of course," Catherine suggested.

"Hmm," was all that Liam could muster at first.

"I think it'll be good for both of us. We are both grieving. We need some sort of company. Even if it's strictly professional."

"Alright, where and what time?" Liam agreed after a few moments of thought.

"How about at six tonight. There is a restaurant a few buildings away from my office; I'm not sure if you've seen it."

"Dine and Live?" He wondered.

"Yes! That's the one. Does that work for you?"

"Yeah, I'll be there," he promised.

"Great, I'll see you at six then," Catherine added before hanging up the phone. As he put the phone down, he wasn't even sure why he agreed. As always, he felt he was being too harsh on Catherine. None of it was her fault; despite her pretty full schedule, she had taken him in and attempted her best to help him. It wasn't her fault he was stubborn and possibly someone who could never be helped. He would go and not give her any attitude. She needed to be able to grieve for the loss of her friend.

* * *

Catherine was already at the restaurant when Liam made it inside. He pointed to her table, and the host led him to it. She was dressed casually, wearing jeans and regular shoes. It helped to let him know it was strictly professional. He took a seat across from her and forced a weak smile.

"How are you doing?" Catherine asked him.

"I'm not sure how to answer that," Liam admitted.

"Well, that's why we are here to talk. I won't even be charging," she joked. Liam once again attempted a smile that quickly faded away.

"You know, it was about ten, maybe eleven years ago, that I first met Stefanie. She was still nineteen, so young. I was twenty-five, still fairly young, with my mental health counseling career. She has always had such a good heart. She has always cared about people so much. I knew she would make for a great therapist one day," Catherine told him. Her eyes were watery and sincere. Liam felt ashamed of himself. How many other people in the world were feeling the way Catherine was at the moment. Worse, how would Stefanie's mother be feeling right now? Despite this time not being his fault, many others in existence were because of his actions.

Liam was unable to say much. There was just too much shame. He felt as if he had never even given Catherine a chance. His mind had always resisted playing along the way he did with Stefanie. Attempting to distract his mind from the negative thoughts, he concentrated on the people. There were few people, which was not a big surprise for a Thursday night. Some appeared to be there on business, others on a date. Some people were on their first date together; it could end up being their only date with each other, or it could lead to everlasting love. The possibilities felt endless. Liam knew too well that he would never have any experience like that.

He had only ever been in one relationship with one woman his entire life, Natalie. That was during an entirely different life, one where he did not have superpowers. Their relationship had ended only a short time before he acquired his powers. Jack McDay was the first supervillain ever in existence. That was also the same man who had attacked the business that Natalie's parents had owned. After the attack, they were forced to move into a different state, forcing the breakup between Liam and Natalie. It had been a hard time for Liam; he had felt anger and thoroughly despised everything about Jack and how he had come to be. He had never bothered to check on how Natalie was doing nowadays. Perhaps he was afraid of what he would find out.

Not too long after their break up, he had followed Jack, and the rest became history. He gained superpowers that would forever make him the worst human being in the world. Now he sat there, right in front of Catherine, the first person he was having dinner with alone for the first time since becoming Faceless. He hated that name, yet he could now see how fitting it was for him. He turned his head and saw the same stranger he had been seeing up ahead. Same long black coat, face still covered by the hoodie. Unlike the other times, this time Catherine was with him. She may be able to confirm to him if this stranger was real or a hallucination.

"Catherine?" Liam said softly.

"Yes?" She responded curiously.

"Behind you, all the way back in that chair, do you see someone with a long black coat and whose face is covered by a hoodie?" Liam casually asked. Catherine turned herself to look at the distance. She turned back to Liam and raised an eyebrow.

"I see nobody over there. I see a vacant table with empty chairs," she answered. Liam was a little puzzled but decided to disregard what he had seen. The two continued to talk. At one point, Catherine spoke about all the times she and Stefanie had hung out for drinks. Liam spoke about his sessions with Stefanie and how paintings had practically become a thing with them. He even revealed that Stefanie had told him to take one of the paintings, which sent Catherine laughing.

"I'm sorry, Liam, I am not laughing in a mean way at all. It's just that it really does sound like something Stefanie would do. She has her own ways of doing things and getting through people, and she doesn't even have to try. It's all-natural to her," Catherine explained.

Throughout the night, his thoughts about Stefanie had been proven true. She cared about people and wanted to help people. She had picked the perfect career to use her ability. Despite Stefanie not having any sort of superpowers, she had the most extraordinary power of all: to make people feel better. They spent a reasonable amount of time in the restaurant. They both took time to eat the main course and even ordered desserts. They both began to share stories about each other until it finally came time for them to depart.

"Are you going to be alright?" Liam asked. Catherine raised an eyebrow, almost feeling insulted.

"Yeah, I will be alright. I go out on my own a lot," she replied. Liam forced a smile.

"Right, sorry, just bad habit," he answered.

"That's alright," she told him. The two returned to their cars, and Liam began driving home.

* * *

Liam was sitting on his couch at about one in the morning when his cell phone began ringing. He quickly looked and saw that it was Catherine calling him. *That's odd.* He thought as he answered the call.

"Hello?" Liam said.

"If it isn't Liam Lewis himself, or should I say Faceless?" A man's voice spoke. The voice was muffled as if it was purposely being distorted.

"Who is this? Where is Catherine?" Liam asked as he felt chills down his spine.

"Why didn't you take her home, Liam? You could have probably gotten lucky tonight," the voice replied.

"WHO IS THIS? WHERE IS CATHERINE?" Liam shouted loudly. The voice began laughing from the other end.

"Catherine is not far from where I am standing. Although, I must say her face may look slightly different now that I have had my boxing practice. Tell you what, Liam, come meet me in the old abandoned factory near your workplace that no one has gone into? Feel free to bring your mask or come as yourself. I honestly don't care."

"IF YOU HURT HER!" Liam sternly shouted. The voice behind the phone began laughing once again.

"If I hurt her, what? You will murder another person? Liam, I know what you are. I know what you have done. Come to the factory, but do not dare go inside, or everyone in it dies. Meet me right outside in the big open parking lot. We will talk there," the voice responded and then hung up. Liam kept the phone next to his ear for a few more seconds. He then slowly lowered his arm and looked at the cell phone. He angrily squeezed his hand so hard that he crushed the phone. He dropped the pieces to the ground and then quickly stormed off, flying through the window in the living room, shattering it to pieces.

Chapter 27

Liam's anger got worse and worse his entire flight. Once he reached the factory, it had reached a whole new level. As he descended into the big parking lot, he saw someone else standing there and staring at the building. It appeared to be the same stranger he had seen with the long coat. However, this person was only wearing a hoodie, and his face was covered by a black snow mask.

The parking lot was empty. After all, the factory had been abandoned for a few years now. The business had gone bankrupt, and no one else had ever purchased the property. It was very secluded without anything around it. It was out of public visibility, so it had become tough to sell the property.

"Liam, you came after all," the voice said. Liam closed his eyes for a few seconds and then reopened them. He wanted to make sure that this was not one of his hallucinations.

"What do you want? Why are you doing this?" Liam asked. He couldn't figure out what the man's plan was, to begin with.

"You really want me to answer that? Are you judging me, Liam? With everything you have done. All the people you have killed. With all the people you have hurt. I have been wondering, Liam, how can you live with yourself?" The stranger told him. The very last words sent him into a shock. He remembered those same exact words from the last villain he had ever faced, the one that authorities had never been able to find. He was, however, one hundred percent certain this couldn't be him.

The only reason why the body of that man had never been found is because Liam had made sure that it wasn't, as a request from his adversary. The man had died. Police had found the body. They just simply had never known it was him they were looking for. They had taken it as just another civilian casualty. Which meant the words were pure coincidence. It was probably the same question that many would come up with.

"Staying quiet, are you Liam? I seem to remember having to witness my little tiny brother see his mother's dead body. And then seeing you there. Do you remember that? When he told you that you killed his mother?" The stranger added. Just like that, the nightmares came back. The young kid standing in front of him, distraught and fearful.

"You killed my mommmyy!" Liam closed his eyes and quickly shook his head. This is what it was all about. Someone who had lost more than just one person. His mother had been lost, and his brother had most likely been traumatized.

"I went into a deep depression at the time, so they took my brother. Gave him to a different home, and I have never been able to see him again. Liam, I will be honest with you right here and right now. I will make you pay and suffer, just as I have in the last couple of years," The stranger warned him. His adversary quickly raised his arm, pointing to the factory's second-floor window. Liam's heart felt as if it would explode at any second. He could see Catherine's mouth covered in tape, tears dripping down her face. Next to her were Tati and Henry. Both of them appeared to be in a panic. Liam was about to charge towards the building, but the stranger quickly spoke up.

"Nah, huh. We aren't done over here just yet, Liam. You listen to what I have to say, and you will listen carefully," the stranger demanded. Liam turned his face towards him. He could feel the wetness in his eyes, attempting to hold back tears.

"Why? Don't punish them. They don't have anything to do with this. It's me, it's all been me," Liam pleaded.

"My mother and brother also had nothing to do with what happened," the stranger iterated. Liam felt a rush of anger going through him. He quickly dashed towards his enemy. His fist was ready, and he swung it when he got close. Only to go through, almost like he was a ghost.

"Thought you would get me so easily?" The voice shouted a few feet away from the other side. Liam stood there, taking a few deep breaths. Then he looked up at the window again. This time, he saw more than just Catherine, Tati, and Henry. There were kids in there, too, running around in panic.

"You have kids up there?" Liam asked in shock.

"Yes, Liam. I have kids, Catherine, your little buddies, and more. As I said, your sins will be paid off by others. You will suffer as I have suffered." the stranger guaranteed.

"You're out of your damn mind!" Liam shouted.

"No, I am not. This is why I started by taking out that bitch, Stefanie," the stranger claimed. Liam's face twitched. Pure hatred took over his own mind. He then looked at the building. He got into position as if he was about to run a track race and then took off, dashing towards the building.

"No. You don't get to have this," the stranger said, lifting a small device with a button and pressing it. The entire building exploded in seconds, knocking Liam back a few feet. He was able to land on his two feet. Once he regained composure, he looked straight ahead and saw the fire burning within the destroyed building. This time, he was unable to hold back the pain and the tears as he collapsed to his knees with his arms wide open while he screamed as loud as he had ever screamed.

He remained in that position, frozen for a few seconds as the flames could be reflected from his eyes. Catherine. Henry. Tati. And many other people he did not know, all gone and dead. Paying for something that none of them had ever been involved in. This... This wasn't right... Hatred, disgust, and anger enveloped Liam. He turned his head and saw that the stranger had also been sent flying back with the blast. He was currently trying to get back up and shake his head.

Before he'd be able to do any more tricks, Liam dashed towards him, grabbed him by the throat, and slammed the stranger's face to the ground. Small drips of blood started coming from the back of the stranger's head. Liam then gathered enough strength in his right arm and punched him in the stomach so hard that his adversary wasn't even able to cry in pain. He then quickly punched him in the face so hard that he literally took the life away from his enemy. After a couple of twitches, the body had no movement or pulse.

Liam let go of the body, and while everything else had felt like a blur before, everything started to clear up. The fire and smoke on the building across were still going. It wouldn't be long now before the police and firemen would arrive. Liam stared at his fist briefly; his stomach felt sick. He then turned towards his dead enemy in shock. He reached out slowly with the same hand and removed the mask.

The feeling became worse. Despite his face being wholly deformed from Liam's punch, he could still see that the man... No, the young boy looked like he was only a teenager. He reached for the teenager's jeans pockets and found a slim wallet. He opened it and was able to see a state I.D. inside it. A greater disgust overwhelmed Liam. He was only sixteen years old. Just sixteen years old. Liam went into a more profound shock as he started breathing heavily. He began to hear the sirens approaching the building. He looked at the kid's right hand and saw the trigger still on top of it.

"You fucked up, you really did. You killed too many innocent people, but now I see that it was me who created the monster. It's all my fault. It's not your legacy that should be tarnished," Liam said without any emotion. He grabbed the trigger and then crushed it with his hand and threw it far away. He flew up high and took off as he heard footsteps approaching the area.

* * *

Back home, Liam stood inside his bathroom, looking down at his sink. Everything was different. The entire world felt different for him. This was the legacy he had created, nothing but pained people all around. All those years that he had thought he was helping, he was doing nothing but creating more immense pain all around. Now, everyone that he had grown close to was gone. Stefanie, Catherine, Henry, Tati, and others inside that abandoned factory were panicking. He slowly raised his head to look straight into the mirror and saw his reflection once more.

Piece of shit. It's all on you; it has always been and will always be. Others will simply try to be nice about it because it is the right thing to do. You are a piece of shit.

He told himself as he stared at the mirror with anger and disgust. The reflection he was looking at was the greatest adversary he had ever faced. His greatest villain. He punched the mirror fiercely. Most of it cracked, while a few pieces fell to the sink. He then left the bathroom, leaving nothing but a distorted reflection of the wall behind him. Just a few seconds later, he returned to the bathroom. Looking at his reflection one more time through the cracked glass.

This was the life he had created. A life of torment for all others, and even Stefanie's death had been because of him, after all. Too many people have died because of him. Too many people had lost loved ones, and too many people had been traumatized and tormented because of him. Being a superhero in the real world was nothing like being a superhero in the comics or movies. It was a much darker path, one that Liam had never anticipated. A path that he had never wanted to go down. At one point, he had been naive, thinking that being a superhero meant saving everyone and making the world happy. Yet, barely a dent had ever been made in this horrible world. His only legacy was that he had created more evil.

He couldn't smile as he focused on his reflection through the cracked mirror. He couldn't admire it. He could only hate it, feel repulsed by it. 'How could he live with himself,' a question he'd been asked multiple times. How could he answer that when 'You killed my mommy' or 'I'll make you suffer as I have' were lines thrown right at him? This was the time to finally do what he should have done long before. It would have saved quite a lot of people today. He then raised his right arm; this time, he was holding a gun. He placed it against his head, and he shed a few more tears with his finger right up against the trigger.

"I am so sorry, world. I wanted to be a hero, and instead, I was a villain," he spoke, and then, just like that, his finger pressed on the trigger, and a loud gunshot echoed across the bathroom.

Chapter 28

The light from the moon reflected inside the hallway just as the main door of the building opened. The footsteps could be heard coming up the flight of stairs. The footsteps stopped when they reached the front of a door, where a large package rested against it. It was rather strange; packages that size were rare at the workplace. The body bent down to pick it up, placed the keys on the door, opened it, and walked inside.

The room looked a little dusty, as if it had been a month since it had been used. Everything else was still the same, including the missing painting ahead. Looking at the couch and the chair around the middle of the room, Stefanie was able to smile. Part of her was glad to be back here, though she would take a couple of days to get settled again from her long trip. Soon enough, she would be seeing her clients again. She smiled as she wondered what Liam may be doing with the painting she had lent him. She approached her chair and then looked at the box.

The sender's name was Liam Lewis. She was confused. Why was Liam sending her mail to her office? It was true that he didn't actually know her home address, but why was he sending a package at all? Wouldn't he soon be seeing her again? Unless he had decided to move away while she was gone. She opened the box curiously and saw that one of the things inside was the same painting she had lent him.

There was also a brown envelope inside, which she quickly opened. She grabbed the inside and removed what was a journal. She was intrigued and, at the same time, a little concerned. What was going on? She opened up to the first page, where she saw the writing.

'Dear Stefanie,

I know you will never get to read this, considering you are no longer in this world. It pains me to think how a reckless drunk driver could just take the life of someone so innocent and kind. Yet, who am I to judge when plenty of times I have been that drunk driver, just simply in different means. Anyhow, when Catherine delivered me the news that you had died, I absolutely had no idea how I would be able to cope with it. I honestly didn't. I have always looked forward to our sessions and was very much looking forward to your return. Your painting has done wonders for me because it reminds me of the sessions and how I can improve myself. I have done so many wrong things that it pains me. I really hope that they can all be forgiven, and perhaps one day you can still have me as a client in the next life if one does exist.

I bought this journal right after our first session but never touched it. Here I am, though. How silly is it that I am writing this for you with the intent of sending it to your office despite knowing you will never get to read it? I guess it's a coping mechanism, or in some way, some sort of closure where I can lie to myself and say that you are alive, and I attempt to move on with life.

I would be lying if I didn't say things have been strange lately. I think I have started to hallucinate, which is quite odd, considering that it had never been an issue before, but as Catherine has made clear, things get bottled up, and things change. Anyway, I wish I could tell you how kind of a person you are and how much you really helped me. Perhaps Catherine's effect has been less significant because I have subconsciously resisted listening to her words. Still, I'll work on that, too.

I will also not lie right now; I think eventually, I will just have to pretend that you are alive in my mind so I can cope with it. I'm unsure how to do it, but I will find a way. I don't want to disappoint you. I don't want to fail you. You are great at your job.

Sincerely,
Liam Lewis.'

Stefanie closed the journal, confused. She put it down on the stand next to her and then leaned back on her chair, trying to figure out how she was dead. She quickly grabbed her phone and searched for the name Liam Lewis on it. There were quite a few results that came up, which surprised her. She expected plenty of results for Faceless, but not Liam. She clicked on one from two days prior.

The article talked about a man who had killed himself in his own house.

After hearing a gunshot, the neighbors called in the police, who arrived on the scene to find the body of Liam Lewis inside the bathroom, with a gun on the ground. He had been lying in a pool of dried blood. Stefanie felt sick to her stomach. What in the world had happened in the one month she was gone? How had it come to this? He was getting better. She could tell he was getting better, or was it simply what she wanted to see?

She continued reading the article where his downstairs neighbor had given a statement. '*I always thought the man wasn't all there in his head. Always making weird sounds from his house, always acting up. I always told my wife that the guy was a psychopath.* Hearing Liam being spoken of that way angered Stefanie. He had gone through a lot and was working through it all. Yet no one would ever realize how pained he truly was. He would be judged, like many others, as either 'too weak,' or 'crazy,' or whatever else people felt like saying.

This was simply not the news she had anticipated upon returning home. What had felt like a positive experience coming to her office now felt clouded by something sinister. She couldn't entirely spin her head on it yet, but she began to reread what Liam had written for her. After going through it several times, she finally picked up her phone and texted. It was time to get answers.

* * *

Stefanie opened the door to the large cafe and looked around, attempting to find someone in particular. Once she managed to find who she was looking for, she slowly walked over to the table. She threw Liam's journal on it without even taking a seat. Puzzled, Catherine reached for the journal on the table.

"What is this?" Catherine asked softly.

"Something Liam wrote to me. Not long before taking his own life," Stefanie firmly told her. Stefanie then took a seat right in front of Catherine. Her face remained as serious as it had ever been. Her usual smile was absent, and the resentment towards Catherine was obvious. She stared at Catherine with a vigorous intensity in her eyes.

"Do you want to explain to me what the fuck happened?" Stefanie coldly demanded.

"I don't know what you're talking about," Catherine responded, pushing the journal back towards Stefanie.

"He was working on himself, trying to erase his nightmares and be his best version. Then you come along and exploit his fragile state of mind," Stefanie spoke angrily.

"I don't know what you mean," Catherine insisted in monotone. Catherine then looked away, avoiding Stefanie's angry gaze at her. Their once strong friendship now felt broken.

"I'm not an idiot, Catherine. Maybe I can't prove it, but I know whatever it was, you did it. You told him I died? Are you out of your fucking mind?" Stefanie spoke a little louder. Catherine looked around the restaurant and noticed a few gazes in their direction. She then quickly turned back to look at Stefanie in the eyes. This time, there was an intense look between the two of them. Catherine's own anger began to come out.

"Do you know that over seventy percent of my clients were living in trauma because they had been affected by the actions of Faceless? Some lost their family members, and some watched people die in person. Others have permanently damaged family members. Kids had to watch their mothers die, and some had to witness family or close friends being dismembered. Over seventy percent of my clients, that is a shit ton of people needing help and counseling because of a supposed superhero," Catherine explained.

"The world isn't back and white, Catherine. Perhaps many got hurt, but many more were saved that could have been victims themselves."

"I do not believe that one bit. Do you know how hard it is to watch people break down, cry, and be in such great and unbearable pain because of what they have lost and seen? I've had to deal with it daily, witnessing it firsthand, session by session. I could feel their pain, their sorrow. No matter what I tried to do or say, it didn't help. I felt helpless and angry," Catherine scorned.

"I have the same job as you, Catherine. I deal with it myself. I do not, however, go around and exploit the fragility in people's minds."

"You see it one way. I see it another way," Catherine responded.

"What happens now if more supervillains are created and no one exists to stop them?" Stefanie asked. Catherine didn't say a word. After moments of silence, Stefanie continued. "We took this job to help people become better. To help people help themselves. Help them be the good person they so desperately want to be. We did not take this job to exploit people's minds and turn them into their greatest adversaries. You should be as disgusted with yourself as I am with you. You should surrender your license and never see any clients again," Stefanie demanded. There was an awkward silence for a few moments before Stefanie continued to speak.

"How did you even do it?"

"Again, Stefanie, I have no idea what you're talking about. I do, however, know I had this young client, aged sixteen, who had abilities himself. He could create illusions, you know," Catherine replied. She leaned back on her chair and began to hear the voices in her head.

"Maybe you shouldn't do this. You can end up dead! Even with your abilities to create illusions, you don't have his strength or bulletproof skin," Catherine told her young client, Nate.

"This needs to be done. His mind is weak already. With my illusions, I made him believe that he was hallucinating. It's all getting to him. You even told me yourself. Plus, if we don't go through with it and Stefanie comes back, we are screwed either way," her client responded.

"What if we go through with it and it still fails? Then Stefanie returns, and everything will be exposed!" Catherine pleaded.

"It will work! You said so yourself. His mind is on a fragile thread right now. One that is easily breakable with the right incentives. Just make him hate himself even more. He's the only one capable of taking his own life," Nate responded calmly.

"Then why that factory? There is no place to hide there! Maybe behind the factory?" Catherine pleaded.

"That factory is good because it is secluded, and no one will be around to risk getting hurt. It has windows as well, which I can make him see whatever I feel like making him see. I also can't be behind the factory because I must physically see him to create the illusions. I also can't go too far away; otherwise, I will lose connection to the trigger for the bomb."

"Just create the illusion of the fire, the explosion."

"Catherine. You know I can't maintain my illusions for long periods. If he does knock me out, the illusion is broken; he will see that the fire never existed. All our plans and my death will have been for nothing," Nate explained.

"I guess. If you are going through this, you must bring it all out. Claim that it was you that killed Stefanie, make him think it was his fault. You wanted him to suffer. Ask him how he can live with himself. It'll draw out more flashbacks," Catherine's voice sounded worried and jittery.

"Roughly two years back, when I saw him getting up from the floor inside my house, his mask was off. I saw his face and have never since forgotten it. My brother walked in to see our mother dead. I was too much of a coward and remained hidden, frozen with fear. He never realized I had seen his face. Then, later on, when he went and destroyed all those labs, I was there. I had been administered a shot of one of their

newer serums. I left just in time before he blew up the entire building. I knew I could never forget his face," the young teenager explained to Catherine.

Catherine's senses returned to the now, where she looked at Stefanie again and forced a cunning smirk. Stefanie wasn't amused. She stood up with her face filled with anger and disgust. Her disgust could probably be felt miles away at that point. She grabbed the journal; she knew that Catherine would never admit it fully or confess.

"I trusted you, and you shit all over me," Stefanie clarified.

"Some are willing to die for the greater cause. Apparently, your client just needed the push for it," Catherine said and smiled. Stefanie started to walk away without ever looking back. Catherine sighed and put both of her hands on her head. Tears began to slip away while her hands trembled.

* * *

The small gathering made Stefanie feel even more sad for Liam Lewis. There were maybe eight other people at his funeral. She gazed around, noticing that two of them must have been Henry and Tati based on what she had learned about them. Two others she guessed to be his mother and father as they stood the closest to the casket, holding each other and crying. Everyone else was probably another relative.

It was the warmest day they had so far, with clear skies. The grass around was well taken care of. The entire cemetery itself looked luxurious. A good place for Liam to finally be able to sleep peacefully. She took a few steps forward, holding a single rose. Before dropping the rose on the casket, she approached his parents and bowed her waist.

"I am sorry if this is out of nowhere, and I hope it's ok that I came. My name is Stefanie. I was his..."

"His therapist," Liam's mom interrupted with a grieving yet gentle smile.

"Yes," Stefanie answered. Her eyes were red and watery; she wanted to scratch them but ignored the itch. She had already done enough crying the night before.

"Liam wrote a letter. He spoke so highly of you. You were helping him. You are a good therapist," his mother added.

"I failed your son. I didn't stop him from... I didn't help him move on," Stefanie reflected as she felt guilty.

"Oh no, don't blame yourself. Liam wrote and spoke to me on the phone several times after he started seeing you. He hadn't had any lengthy conversations with us before. After starting to go to the sessions, he reached out to us for the first time in a long while. I could tell he was getting so much better. Something else must have happened; he must have had one bad day, and unfortunately, sometimes it's all it takes," his mother replied. More guilt enveloped Stefanie. She clenched her hands and teeth, knowing precisely what had happened, at least part of it. Even if Catherine hadn't admitted to her, she could tell in her former friend's attitude and face. Catherine had manipulated Liam, taking advantage of his very own nightmares and demons. He had trusted them by making himself vulnerable.

Stefanie still blamed herself as she had been the one who referred him to Catherine. She had looked up to and trusted her and, in the end, had been betrayed. She couldn't quite say anything to anyone without revealing Liam's identity as Faceless. Considering the world was divided on their feelings of Faceless, it was better if no one knew who he was. If word ever got out that Faceless was dead, who knows what that could lead to. More villains hidden in the shadows? Tempering with Liam's grave? There was no way of knowing; he deserved to rest in peace and be left alone. That upset Stefanie even more, knowing that Catherine would retain her license despite malpractice, but Liam needed to sleep peacefully. She spent some quiet moments with his parents as they bid their farewells.

* * *

In her house, Stefanie sat on her back patio. Her laptop was open and resting on the table while her legs stretched onto another seat. There was a glass of wine right next to the laptop, and for a few moments, she admired her backyard, which had recently been taken care of. A squirrel was maneuvering around, unable to decide whether to climb the tree or stay on the grass. The world may slowly heal itself. Maybe the world would forget Liam, even if it never forgot Faceless. However, it was never Faceless that she had met; she had met Liam, and she would never forget that the man behind the mask was going through his own inner battles. She would continue to do what she was doing: helping people.

She couldn't allow guilt to hold over her. It was Catherine who should be ashamed of her actions. Stefanie was determined to become better and help people more. The world may not always be full of light. Still, at that particular moment, sunlight illuminated her backyard as if it were a world of its own. On her laptop screen was a search for places where she could adopt a dog.

Suicide is not a joke and should be taken serious. You never know what someone might be going through, or has gone through. If you or someone you know is showing signs or having thoughts of suicide please seek out help.

Suicide Prevention Hotline

988

For more information visit:

https://suicidepreventionlifeline.org

You are important, you do matter.

Don't you ever forget that!

Wounds of a Super Hero

by

Andre Pereira

About the Author(Me):

Hello everyone! I was born as a baby, as opposed to something else of course, in Lisboa, Portugal. At the age of ten years old is when I moved to the United States with my family. Obviously, moving to a whole new country that young without knowing the language at all presented a few challenges. All of which I overcame. I learned English within a year, and there I was going.

Ever since I was really young, I have always loved movies, or any sort of story. Can't quite explain it, but it's just something it always enamored me. Which is why I'm capable of watching just about any genre of movies, including movies which people consider terrible.

At a young age I started joining anime forums, and from there I began writing fan-fiction. Looking back at those stories now, I can see that characters had little depth at the time. Then in seventh and eight grade, I wrote a few fiction stories in my English class. Honestly, I'm glad I didn't scare the teacher with all those slasher horror stories. Though, I turned out quite alright.

In my life I have dealt with major depression, generalized anxiety, trauma and so on. Thus I became interested and very big on mental health awareness. Not afraid to admit it, I went through some very rough times, but I got through them. I did seek out therapy and still attend therapy despite feeling the best I've felt in long long time.

Majority of my stories will contain some sort of genre such as fantasy, supernatural, mystery, etc.... The one thing they all have in common is that they deal heavily with characters mental state, their struggles, non struggles, and etc... I like it to be character driven and walk through the grey area of the world. None of my stories are meant to glorify any negative effects from any illness. It is meant to bring it out into the open so that people can understand what others may be going through, how rough it can be.

When I'm not writing or working full time, I am either watching television, playing kickball, going out with friends, or going out by myself, because one should be able to enjoy their own company.

Sign up for my mailing newsletter at:

Positivezeropublishing.com

In here you will be able to receive news, updates, chances to win prizes as well as signed copies of future novels.

Like the Facebook page as well:
@pzpublishing

Like the Instagram Page:
@positivezeropublishings

Also by Andre Pereira:
Blurred Memories (Psychological Thriller)
Written as Hybrid of Script

Future:

The New Gods Trilogy
Stellar Darkness Second Story
Andre Presents: A Walk in the Darkness

Follow on Facebook and Insta and sign up for newsletters for more news and updates regarding the other stories in the future.

Milton Keynes UK
Ingram Content Group UK Ltd.
UKHW011122180424
441376UK00004B/162